The Big Score

The Big Score

By

Sa'Neal

TATE PUBLISHING
AND ENTERPRISES, LLC

Published by Tate Publishing & Enterprises, LLC
127 E. Trade Center Terrace | Mustang, Oklahoma 73064 USA
1.888.361.9473 | www.tatepublishing.com

Tate Publishing is committed to excellence in the publishing industry. The company reflects the philosophy established by the founders, based on Psalm 68:11,
"The Lord gave the word and great was the company of those who published it."

Published in the United States of America

ISBN: 978-1-68187-319-0
1. Fiction/ General
2. Fiction/ African American/General
15.04.21

Chapter One

It is graduation night and the Allen Family along with the Johnson family has thrown their children Harrison and Bahari a party together. They are both high achievers, Harrison a basketball player and an "A" student. Bahari is a cheerleader and also an "A" student. They are both popular at their high school and were voted "Couple of the Year" and Bahari, "Most likely to succeed" and Harrison won "Most Athletic."

Both sets of parents have spared no expense on the graduation party and the kids are all having a good time. Both parents are hoping to one day be one "Big Happy Family" when Harrison asks for Bahari's hand in marriage. The kids have always liked each other from the time the parents met when they were both toddlers, they did everything together and now they will be going off to college together.

They were both accepted into Duke University, Harrison for his athletic ability and Bahari for her academic ability, they both got full scholarships, which made both sets of parents proud. They are both from Trinidad and a lot is placed on them academically from both sets of parents. Bahari's parents are both Doctors.

1

Harrison's father is a heart surgeon and his mother a stay-at-home Mom, she quit her job as a therapist when Harrison was born.

"I am so glad we are going to school together, it would have been weird going to separate schools," said Harrison with a smile.

"I know I was on pins and needles until I got my acceptance letter, I am just ready for summer break then get back into my studies," says Bahari.

"I won't have a break I got to practice all summer, but I will spend time with you, I'll make sure of it," says Harrison trying to reassure her.

"You better," says Bahari as she punches him on his bicep.

Bahari has an athletic build, five foot six, long dark brown hair, dark skin and dimples, most people say she looks a lot like Jennifer Hudson (after the weight loss) because of her curvy hips and infectious smile.

Harrison is six foot six, dark skinned, athletic build and he sports a low even all over haircut.

When the party winds down and all the guest are gone Bahari and Harrison sneak off in the backyard of Harrison's parents house into the tree house his and her father built when they were eight years old to have a moment to themselves. Bahari lives in the next subdivision over.

1

"When do you have to leave for Duke," says Bahari.

"In a week," says Harrison as he looks her in the eyes.

"How long are you going to be gone?" asks Bahari.

"For six weeks, but my parents said that you can come up with them when they come to visit to sit in on a few of the practices," says Harrison.

"I hope my parents let me go," says Bahari.

"They will," says Harrison.

"I'll miss you," says Bahari as she lowers her head.

Harrison takes his hand and places it on her chin and raises her head and gives her kiss.

"I will miss you too, that time will pass quickly then we will be there together," says Harrison as he gives her a soft peck on the lips.

They hug each other without saying a word.

"Bahari, Harrison, where are you?" asks Bahari's mother as she is calling out their names for them to return to the house.

They are looking down on her from the tree house searching the yard and giggling with their hands covering their mouths.

"SHHHH," says Harrison.

Harrison kisses her again, but this time passionately.

When Mrs. Johnson goes back into the house they climb down from the tree house and go back into Harrison's home.

The Allen's have a huge home of fifty-two hundred square feet, decorated with an island feel, with tennis courts, a pool, five bedrooms, six baths, chef's kitchen, theatre room, and a study.

"There you are I was outside calling for you," says Mrs. Johnson with a worried look.

"I didn't hear you, Mom," says Bahari and she walks over to her mother and gives her a hug.

"She was safe, she was with me," says Harrison with a smile and he winks at Bahari.

"This is for you," says Mrs. Allen.

"It's from me and your Dad," as she hands him a beautifully wrapped Cartier box.

Harrison pulls the bow off of it and opens the box and he sees a Cartier watch inside.

"Mom, Dad this is so nice, thank you," says Harrison.

"It's about time you had a real timepiece son, so take care of it," says Mr. Allen.

Harrison puts the watch on and walks over to Bahari to show it to her.

"Here is your gift baby from me and your father," says Mrs. Johnson with a smile as she hands Bahari a box.

Bahari opens the beautifully wrapped Tiffany's box and sees a tennis bracelet.

"I always wanted one just like you momma," says Bahari as she admires the bracelet.

Bahari's father Kenneth walks over to Bahari and takes it out of the box and places it on her wrist.

"You are growing up, but you will always be my little girl," says Kenneth in his island accent.

"Oh my goodness, Kenneth have you looked at her lately, she is a woman," says Mrs. Johnson.

"Thanks Mom and Dad, I love you guys," says Bahari.

"You guys are the best parents," says Harrison.

"Yes, I am happy that they are OUR parents," says Bahari with a smile.

Both kids hug their parents.

Mrs. Allen goes to the refrigerator to retrieve a bottle of wine for a toast.

Mr. Allen gets the wine glasses.

After Mrs. Allen pours everyone a glass and gets the kids a soda they do a toast.

"We are so proud of the both of you and we will all miss you when you leave for college, you won't be our babies anymore. It is time we let you go and make your way in the world, together of course (as she looks at Harrison and Bahari). Look out Duke because Harrison Allen and Bahari Johnson are coming," says Mr. Allen with a raised glass then everyone takes a sip.

After being at the Allen's home until the wee hours of the morning, the Johnson family returns to their home.

Harrison has left for practice with the Duke Basketball team and Bahari is happy because her parents have agreed to let Bahari accompany the Allen's on a trip over the summer to visit Harrison for the weekend. She and Harrison would normally be spending the summer going to movies, arcades and the two families would have taken a trip together, but this year they are going to save a vacation for the Christmas holidays instead because of their rigorous schedules.

When Bahari arrives in Durham, North Carolina with Harrison's parents she is relieved, the trip seemed to have taken forever. She was excited to see Harrison it had been a month since they saw each other, just late night phone calls and calls in between practices, this had been the longesttime that she and Harrison had been separated since they've known each other.

From the airport they go straight to the hotel to check-in then to Duke University to see Harrison and the team practice. She was elated when she walked into the gym and spotted him.

Though she has seen Harrison practice and play in games many times before, it was nice to see him sweaty and forcibly handling the ball which made his muscles flex and made her smile.

After practice Harrison goes and takes a shower then he meets his parents and Bahari at the front of the Duke gymnasium.

"Hi Mom, Dad," says Harrison as he gives his parents a hug.

"Hi, Son," says Harrison's parents in unison.

"Hi Bahari," says Harrison with a smile and he kisses her on the cheek.

They are both excited to see each other, but they must contain themselves in front of Harrison's parents.

"You hungry?" asks Mr. Allen.

"Yes, where are we going?" asks Harrison.

"I saw an Olive Garden on the way here a few miles back towards the hotel," says Mrs. Allen.

"Cool," says Harrison as he adjusts his duffle bag on his shoulder.

"So what have you been up to?" asks Harrison of Bahari as they walk to the car.

"Bored and getting ready to come to school, just a few more weeks and I'll be here too," says Bahari with a smile.

"How do you like it so far?" asks Bahari as they get into the Cadillac Escalade that the Allen's have rented.

Harrison throws his duffle bag in the back seat.

"It's cool haven't really done anything or had a social life because we are having two-a-days and when I am not practicing I am sleeping, eating or just relaxing with the rest of the team," says Harrison.

"You sure you gonna be able to handle your schedule when classes start?" asks Bahari.

"Yes, I just got to stay focus and do what I got to do," says Harrison as he adjusts himself in his seat.

"Bahari, are you going to join any organizations or cheerlead in the fall?" asks Mrs. Allen.

"No, I just want to get my head around my studies and see how I can balance classes and studying," says Bahari.

When they arrive at the Olive Garden they all take a seat and order food, they talk, laugh and enjoy each other company. After they finished their meal they head to the hotel it has been a long day for all of them, they are tired.

When they arrive back at the hotel the Allen's have a two-bedroom suite and Bahari has a suite of her own.

Bahari is in her suite alone, she has showered and was relaxing watching television when she heard a knock on the door.

"Yes," says Bahari.

"It's me open the door," says Harrison.

Bahari opens the door to Harrison standing there with a big smile on his face.

"Hey, baby," says Harrison.

"Hey, I was so happy to see you today," says Bahari with a smile as she reaches up to give Harrison a kiss.

Harrison takes her in his arms while he kisses and holds her tightly.

"Me too, you looked so nice, you put a few pounds on," says Harrison.

"I know I haven't been exercising like usual but what are you saying, Harrison," asked Bahari with her hands on her hips.

"Oh, nothing, I like it as long as you don't lose those curves," says Harrison with a smile.

They take a seat on the couch in the living room of the suite and order a pay-per-view movie, Madea goes into Witness Protection.

They laughed, snacked on almond joys and popcorn that Bahari brought from home and talked about the upcoming school year at Duke.

When it got around one o' clock in the morning there was a knock on the door.

"Yes," says Bahari.

"It's Mr. Allen," says Mr. Allen.

When Bahari answers the door Mr. Allen steps inside and looks around.

"Harrison, it is time for you to go. You need to get your rest," says Mr. Allen.

"Okay, goodnight Bahari," says Harrison in a low tone voice then he gets up off the couch, gives Bahari a hug and leaves to return to his suite.

"Goodnight, what time should I be up in the morning," says Bahari.

"Come to our room at eight sharp we will go downstairs together for breakfast, get some sleep," says Mr. Allen.

"Okay," says Bahari as she closes the door behind them.

Bahari turns the television off in the living room area and goes into the bedroom, wraps her hair, says her prayers and gets into bed.

Bahari misses Harrison already and hates she has to spend the night alone. She often dreams of their first night together as husband and wife, they are both virgins and have vowed to stay that way until their wedding night.

Bahari is almost asleep when her cell phone rings.

"Hello."

"Hey, are you asleep?"

"No, I miss you."

"I miss you too, I wanted to stay I didn't want to leave you."

"That would have been nice."

"You are going to get into trouble if your dad catches you on the phone."

"They are in their room with the door closed."

After breakfast I want to take you for a walk on campus if my Mom and Dad will let us have a moment alone. It's beautiful here."

"I'd like that."

"My mom wants to go to the mall."

"I figured that, but I ain't mad at her."

"I can't wait until we can spend all the time we want together."

"Me too, when school starts we can do what we want."

"I know."

"I love you."

"I love you too; I need to go so I can wake up in the morning."

"Bye, see you in the morning."

"Bye."

They both release the line.

Bahari turns over and goes to sleep thinking about Harrison and her wedding night

Harrison can't wait for the fall term to begin so that they may be together.

Chapter Two

The Allen's and the Johnson families are on the Duke campus to get Bahari and Harrison ready for the fall term at school. Mrs. Johnson has made Bahari's favorites and packaged them in Tupperware bowls and put them into her tiny dormitory refrigerator and she even made a few of Harrison's favorites and gave them to him. The Allen's has given Harrison gift cards to most of the restaurants in the area along with a few meals that Mrs. Allen has prepared for him.

The Allen's are in the athletic dorms moving Harrison's things in and The Johnson's are moving in Bahari's things. It's a bittersweet time for both parents it will be lonely when they return to Chicago without the kids in both residences. It will never be the same in either residence without their hectic schedules, the neighborhood kids running around in the house, the sleepovers and all the nervous energy that comes along with having kids in the house.

After they are both moved in and they have met their roommates the two families go to dinner then back to their hotels.

It is Sunday morning the parents are saying their goodbyes to the kids and wish them well for the fall term and remind them that they are there for an education and NOT the parties, though they know there will be plenty of parties.

It is "Welcome Week" on campus and there are parties all day and into the night on campus. Bahari is not much of a partier, but she is away from home and everyone is doing it, she has even had a drink at one of the parties, it was just a beer, but she felt guilty about it and she didn't even like the taste. Harrison laughed at the way she frowned when she took a sip of the beer, he drank his like a pro, Harrison's father often has beer in the house and he has had a sip or two when his father wasn't looking and he actually likes it. He's more of a fan of imported beer and not Budweiser, which seems to be a college favorite.

By Friday night from all the partying and hanging out until the wee hours of the morning Bahari and Harrison were beginning to feel like things were getting a little wild and knew they need to slow it down and get ready for classes the following week. The weekend they stayed in and watched movies at night instead of going to parties, they were both a little worried about the first day of school because they knew they were going to have to study harder than when in High School because now they were in the big leagues and only the cream will rise to the top.

The first week of classes were hard for both Harrison and Bahari and they had to study so much that they hardly got to see each other, but it was Friday, the first weekend was upon them and they were both looking forward to it.

They were meeting with some friends of Harrison's from the team at Bullock's Bar-B-Q they said the portions are big and it's a place you got to visit when visiting Durham, North Carolina.

The place has a country feel and the servers are country, but nice all at the same time.

They ate on a wooden table with benches for chairs, they feasted on hand pulled pork sandwiches, ribs, French fries, coleslaw, baked beans, greens and for dessert Bahari and Harrison shared a piece of Snicker bar pie.

After the gang of eight finished dinner they all went to the movies then they all split up and went their separate ways.

"Did you enjoy yourself?" asks Harrison when they get back into his Mustang.

"I did your friends are nice," says Bahari as she is yawning.

"You sleepy?" asks Harrison.

"A little, it's been a long week," says Bahari as she covers her mouth.

"Yeah, for me too," says Harrison.

Bahari looks at her watch.

"I got to get back to the dorms," says Bahari. "I know, me too," says Harrison.

"Are you worried about not being able to keep up with your classes because I am starting to feel the pressure," says Harrison.

"A little, but I can only do my best and so should you," says Bahari.

"I know, but I am starting to feel overwhelmed already," says Harrison.

"I know how you feel, I have a ton of homework and this is only the first week," says Bahari.

"It was easier in high school because the teachers kind of gave you a pass being an athlete, but here I get the feeling there will be no passes," says Harrison with a worried look.

"Harrison, you worry all the time and score higher than anybody on any given test. You will be fine," says Bahari.

As they pull up to the dorm rooms where Bahari resides, Bahari can't wait to get into bed she is exhausted.

"See you tomorrow," says Harrison as the car comes to a stop.

"Yes, of course," says Bahari with a smile and she yawns again.

They both laugh out loud.

"Get some sleep," says Harrison with a smile as he reaches over to give her a kiss.

"I will, you too," says Bahari.

They kiss and Bahari exits the car, she waves goodbye and Harrison drives away feeling good because she always supports him and makes him feel good about himself.

The next few weeks of school is getting better for the both of them they are both getting into a study routine that is demanding, but necessary.

"Bahari we are all going down to the library, you want to go?" asks Bahari's roommate Toni.

"No, I am going to study alone for a little while longer," says Bahari as she looks up from her textbook just for a second to smile at her roommate.

"Pierre is going to be there," says Toni with a smile.

"I keep telling him that Harrison and I are dating and he keeps coming at me, he is a cutie though with them hazel eyes," says Bahari with a smile.

"I know I keep telling him that too, but he won't listen. He is chasing quite a few of the girls on campus, but he really likes you," says Toni.

"Well he can get his mind off me because this chic is taken. I have been in love with Harrison since we were kids," says Bahari as she turns the page of her textbook.

"Have you ever dated anyone else?" asks Toni.

"Nope, our families are really close and besides I have never even wanted to date someone else," says Bahari.

"Wow, girl I have had about four boyfriends, how do you know what you want, if you have never been with anybody else?" asks Toni with a funny look on her face.

"I just know and just so you know, I am still a virgin. I am going to wait until my wedding night," says Bahari in a matter-of-fact tone.

"You better than me, well have fun studying, I'll call you on the way back if we stop and get something to eat I'll call to see if you want anything," says Toni as she checks her hair and makeup in the mirror one last time before she grabs her bag full of books and walks out the door.

"Okay, thanks," says Bahari as she gets up to lock the door.

Bahari turns her attention to her books and after a few hours she decides to go to bed.

Around midnight her cell phone rings.

"Hello," says Bahari in a sleepy voice.

"I miss you," says Harrison.

I miss you too," says Bahari as she sits up in bed and notices her roommate still has not made it back yet.

"I went to the library I saw Toni, why didn't you come?" asks Harrison.

"I just wanted to study peacefully alone, these classes are kicking my butt," says Bahari.

"We could have studied together," says Harrison.

"Why didn't you call me?" asks Bahari.

"I didn't want to disturb you," says Harrison.

"You are never disturbing me," says Bahari.

"I just wanted to check on you, I need to get some sleep I got an English Lit test tomorrow that I need to do well on and a biology test after that," says Harrison.

"Okay I will call you in the morning, can we do lunch together?" asks Bahari.

"Yes, I will call you," says Harrison.

"Okay, talk to you tomorrow. I love you," says Bahari.

"Love you too," says Harrison.

They both release the line.

Bahari hears the key in the door and in walks Toni and she smells as if she has been drinking.

"What up Roomy," says Toni giggling.

"Toni have you been drinking?" asks Bahari in an authoritative voice.

"Yes, I have. After we left the library we went to Pierre's apartment and had a few beers. He said to tell you to leave them jocks alone," says Toni as she plops down on her bed and starts to undress.

"Girl, don't tell me nothing he has to say, he is so silly. He is just jealous of Harrison, I hear the things he says about him behind his back," says Bahari.

"He is a hater though, but speaking of Harrison I saw him with Amanda at the library they were all cozy studying together," says Toni.

"I just talked to Harrison and he said he was alone at the library," said Bahari.

"And they left together," says Toni.

"He probably just gave her a ride," says Bahari dismissing the idea the he could be cheating on her.

"I saw them turn into the McDonalds for a midnight snack," says Toni in a snappy tone.

"Toni go to bed, I am not about to let this bother me. Harrison is a nice guy and they probably just got something to eat then he dropped her off at the dorms I am sure it was harmless," says Bahari.

"You got to watch that girl, they go after these ball players especially the white girls," says Toni.

"I am not worried about that, Harrison loves me and that is all I got to say about that, now go to bed, goodnight Alchy," says Bahari as she turns her back to Toni and tries hard to fall asleep. The information that Toni just shared with her is bothering her, but she refuses to let Toni know it.

(The next day)

Bahari and Harrison have lunch at the Pizzeria on campus.

"Are you still nervous about your test?" asks Bahari.

"Nah, I have studied all I can I think I can pass it," says Harrison with a smile as he takes a sip of his soda.

"I got a test today in Anatomy at four, I am feeling confident too," says Bahari as she takes a bite of her pizza.

"Can I see you later," informs Harrison.

"I would like th--," says Bahari, but was cut off mid-sentence.

"Hello Harrison," says Amanda waving as she passes the table where Bahari and Harrison are seated.

"Hi, Amanda," says Harrison.

"Thanks for helping me last night with my math," says Amanda with a smile.

"No problem," says Harrison.

"You think you can tutor me?" asks Amanda with a devilish smile. She doesn't even acknowledge Bahari at the table.

"No, I have basketball season coming up and practice starts in two weeks," says Harrison.

"Well if you change your mind, you got my number," states Amanda.

"Okay, see you later," says Harrison as Amanda walks away.

"You didn't even acknowledge me Harrison, what was up with that?" asks Bahari.

"I'm sorry," says Harrison as he takes a bite of his pepperoni pizza.

"You told me you were studying alone at the library," adds Bahari.

"I was until she came to the table asking me to help her with some math homework she had," says Harrison as he chews his pizza.

"I also heard you guys went to McDonalds afterwards, why was she in your car?" asks Bahari in a slightly angry tone.

"She was in my car because when she told me she walked to the library, I offered to take her back to the dorms. I didn't want her walking by herself at night and we stopped by McDonald's because I was hungry," says Harrison starting to feel a little under attack.

"She is always looking at me like I am crazy or something when I see her on campus," says Bahari as she takes a sip of her drink.

"Baby don't worry about her, she is just a friend," says Harrison as he reaches over and tries to give her a kiss on the cheek.

Bahari moves out of the way.

"I ain't feeling that way right now, you lied to me," says Bahari as she looks at him.

"Babe I didn't lie, I just didn't tell you," says Harrison in a sincere tone.

"Are we keeping secrets now?" asks Bahari with a raised eyebrow.

"No, she is just a friend I gave a ride, you are the woman I love," says Harrison with a smile.

Harrison tries to kiss her again and this time she reciprocates.

"Make sure it doesn't happen again," says Bahari.

"I will Mrs. Johnson, scouts honor," says Harrison as he sits up straight in his seat.

"Okay," says Bahari with a smile.

They finish their lunch and say goodbye to get ready for the remainder of their classes for that day.

Chapter Three

It is the first rival game of the season for Duke University and there is a packed house. Harrison's parents are there and so is Bahari's they are all sitting in the stands together.

"I am so excited, we are going to win this game," says Bahari with a smile.

"They look ready," says Mrs. Allen as she passes some popcorn to her husband.

"They have an awesome team so I have no doubt that they will get a win tonight and start the season off right," says Mr. Allen.

"Harrison looks as if he has put on more muscle," observes Mrs. Johnson.

"That's because of all the practicing, they really work these guys physically," says Mr. Allen.

Its tip-off time and the game began.

In the first half Harrison has six points and they are winning by four.

The second half Harrison has twenty-eight points and there are two minutes left in the quarter. Harrison steals the ball from his opponent and throws it down the court to a teammate and he throws the ball up for a two-pointer, Duke Won the game by two points at the buzzer and the crowd goes wild and runs out onto the court.

The Allen's and the Johnson's go crazy as they run onto the court to congratulate their son, he has twenty-eight points and several assist.

After the game they are all waiting for Harrison when Bahari sees him walking with Amanda and some other white girls laughing. Bahari is fuming she walks over to where he is and grabs his arm.

"Hey, I am so proud of you, great game baby," says Bahari.

"Hey, thanks," says Harrison.

"Are you coming to the party later," says a white girl that Bahari does not know.

"No, I am going to be with the family, my mom and dad came down for the game maybe next time," informs Harrison.

"You sure," asks the girl.

"Yes, he's sure," says Bahari in a matter-of-fact tone.

"I was asking him," says the girl.

"I know and I answered," says Bahari.

"She's right, I'll see you later Darla," says Harrison.

The white girl and the rest of her groupie friends walk off giggling.

"Harrison these groupies are starting to get on my nerves," informs Bahari.

"I don't know why you let them bother you, I ain't thinking about them girls, they are just that, GROUPIES," says Harrison.

"Well I don't like it," says Bahari.

"Hey, I got to get to the locker room I'll meet you guys out front after I changed. I'm hungry," says Harrison as he walks away trying to act as if he is not annoyed by Bahari's jealousy.

After Harrison gets changed and the two families go out and eat they enjoy the rest of the weekend that consisted of; shopping, dining and movies.

A few weeks later

"I am worried about Harrison," says Bahari with a worried look.

"Why?" asks Toni as she looks up from her textbook.

"I am concerned about all the attention he is getting from all these other girls on campus, some girl is always in his face when I see him and it is starting to get to me. This Darla girl is really starting to get on my last nerves and she does it to irritate me," says Bahari.

"He loves you and you know thatwomenes come along with the territory. Womenes are always going to spread their legs for athletes so I suggest you grow a thick skin if you want to be with him," says Toni in a serious tone as she shifts in her chair.

"I am starting to doubt the way he feels because lately he is spending more time with his friends and teammates," says Bahari.

"He can't spend every waking moment with you, he is a jock and they do jock things like; hang out, play their video games together, flirt and most of all practice. College changes relationships. I was in love when I got to Duke and I thought he loved me, but he wanted to be single. This campus is huge and there is so much competition especially from the white womenes," says Toni.

"I know they come on so strong, what is a man to do. They are willing to wash their clothes, do their homework, cook and give them head. The black girls they will just have sex with them because you know we are not going to clean nothing, let alone cook for their lazy asses," says Bahari with a smile.

The two girls slap hands in agreement while giggling.

"Girl you are going to be okay because Harrison is a good guy and he is so polite. I have seen you guys together he loves you. Don't let these womenes throw you off your game," says Toni with a smile.

"It just gets on my nerves and sometimes I think he enjoys the attention," says Bahari as she shuffles through some papers on her desk.

"What man wouldn't, but Harrison doesn't want a groupie he wants you. Y'all have known each other since you were kids. I just better get an invite to the wedding no matter where I am in the world because I have no intentions of returning to Alabama when I graduate. I am going to live in a big city somewhere," says Toni.

"I'd like to go back to live in Chicago, but I have the feeling that Harrison's career is going to take us somewhere else, but I don't care as long as we are together," says Bahari.

"Hey you are bringing me down, let's go shopping at the mall," says Toni as she slams shut her textbook.

"Cool, I guess so because I am getting nothing done anyway, my mind is occupied," says Bahari as she stands up from her desk and starts to straighten the papers on it.

"Did something happen and that's what has you upset?" asks Toni.

"No, he didn't do anything in particular just when we are together girls are always coming up to him is all," says Bahari.

"You know you can't stop these womenes from coming up to him," says Toni as she opens the closet door to choose an outfit to wear to the mall.

"I know, but sometimes he doesn't acknowledge me and he says because they are nobody just groupies," says Bahari.

"Well then what are you worried about?"I told you Harrison is smart and he sees what is going on, I bet he won't let anyone disrespect you," says Toni as she fumbles through her closet.

"I don't know, maybe I am worried about nothing. Let's go get some clothes therapy," says Bahari with a smile on her face and she seems to be cheering up.

"I hear that," says Toni as she pulls a pair of jeans out the closet along with a sweater and a scarf.

After dressing the two women head to the mall in Bahari's fully loaded white Infinity G Convertible, which was given to her as a Christmas present.

When they arrive at the mall it is crowded, they head straight for Forever 21 their favorite store. It is crowded and they see a few fellow students in the store.

"That's why I don't like to come here sometimes because everyone buys their clothing from here," says Bahari as she looks through a few sports jackets on a rack.

"I know, but this is what I can afford," says Toni as she looks at a dress hanging on a rack then she throws it over her shoulder.

"I am trying this on," says Toni.

"Okay, you do that all the time, you grab the first thing you see in the store and besides, Misty has that same dress, she has the blue one," says Bahari.

"Oh, she sure does," says Toni then she puts it back on the rack.

"She would swear you were copying her if you bought that," says Bahari.

"You are right, she makes me so sick always bragging about what she has," says Toni.

"That girl ain't got anything because when you got it you don't talk about it," says Bahari as she checks out a pair of sweat pants and she takes them off the rack and throws them over her arm.

"Hey look to your left, there is Darla and her gang," says Toni.

"Oh, really, she is always with a group of girls she is never by herself," informs Bahari as she spots her across the store.

"She talks so much crap about people that she needs her posse to keep her from being jumped and she is always messing with someone else's man," says Toni as she eyes Darla from the corner of her eye.

"You right about that," says Bahari as she picks up a v-neck white shirt then another pair of sweatpants, but in a different color.

The two women walk over to another side of the store and make a few more choices in clothing to take into the dressing room so that they may try them on.

When they get to the dressing room Darla is waiting in line.

Toni and Bahari decide not to speak unless she speaks to them, but they knew that she would speak just so that she could be nosey.

"Hey, I didn't see you guys," says Darla.

"Hi," says Bahari as she shuffles the clothes in her arms.

"Hi," says Toni in a low tone.

"What are y'all up to today, y'all going to the frat party tonight at the Omega house," says Darla with a smile.

"I haven't made up my mind I have a ton of homework," says Bahari.

"Me, too, but don't be surprised if you see me there," says Toni.

"How is Harrison?" asks Darla with a grin.

"He is fine Darla," says Bahari in a crass tone.

"I know that, I asked how he is doing?" says Darla as she gives one of her friends the high five.

"Why do you have to be rude all the time?" asks Bahari.

"I am just giving you your props," says Darla as she looks over at her friend and the both let out a little giggle.

"You know he is my boyfriend I don't want to hear that stuff," says Bahari in an irritated tone.

The host at the dressing room takes Darla's items and escorts her into a dressing room.

"We will see about that college has a way of making a man re-evaluate puppy love," says Darla as she walks into the dressing room with a devilish smile on her face.

"See she wants me to get ignorant with her, but I am not going to let her get to me," says Bahari.

Darla's friend follows her into the dressing room with a smirk on her face.

"I know just ignore her," says Toni.

After waiting another few minutes Toni and Bahari are shown to separate dressing rooms.

After making their purchases, they go to Dillards and Macy'sthen they go to the food court to grab a bite to eat.

They decide on eating at the Panda.

They grab a table near the center of the food court as they are chattering and enjoying their food, Toni sees Harrison and some of his teammates walking into the food court Bahari can't see them because she is facing the other direction. .

"What did Harrison say he was doing today?" asks Toni as she puts a piece of chicken into her mouth.

"He said he was going to hit the gym earlier take a nap then play some video games or whatever with the fellas and later he and I are going to the movies," responds Bahari as she takes a sip of her Sprite.

"Well he just walked into the food court with about six members of the basketball team," says Toni as she points in Harrison's direction.

Bahari pauses then she stands to wave Harrison over to where she is sitting.

Harrison sees her and hits the other guy on the shoulder that is standing next to him.

"Hey Boo," says Harrison as he reaches down to give Bahari a kiss.

The rest of the team says hello and they all pull up chairs.

"Hi Tony, wassup," says Greg one of Harrison's teammates.

"Hey Greg, what are y'all up to?" asks Toni with a smile.

"Just hanging out," says Greg.

"What did you buy me?" asks Harrison as he looks into Bahari's bag.

"Nothing (pause) just joking I got you a shirt," says Bahari as she reaches into her Macy's bag and pulls out a white Nike shirt with blue writing and hands it to Harrison.

Harrison unfolds the shirt.

The shirt has a message on the front that says; All I Do Is Ball with a picture of a basketball player dunking a basketball.

"Thanks babe," says Harrison and he kisses her on the cheek.

"Did you decide on a movie yet?" asks Harrison.

"Twilight Saga; Breaking Dawn 2," said Bahari as she takes some lo mein into her mouth.

"I forgot that was out," says Harrison as he takes Bahari's fork and takes a bite of her food.

"We have seen each of them I started to get t-shirts, but I thought that would be a little cheesy," says Bahari with a smile.

Harrison reaches for her drink and takes a sip.

"It would have been," says Harrison as he takes some more of her food into his mouth.

"You guys mind if me and Tony joined you guys," says Greg as he looks over at Toni.

"Are you asking me on a date?" asks Toni.

"I don't know are you coming?" says Greg with a sly grin.

"I gotta check my schedule," says Toni as she pulls out her phone and pretends to be checking her calendar.

"It seems that I am free," says Toni with a smile.

"Yeah, I think it would be fun," says Bahari.

"Let's do it," says Harrison as he eats more of Bahari's food.

"Baby if you are hungry I can go and get you some," says Bahari in a sarcastic tone.

"Why would I do that, I got yours," says Harrison with a grin as he slides her plate in front of him.

"Hey man, we are about to go for a walk ya'll gonna catch up later," says the other four guys that Harrison is with.

"Not sure, I'll call you on your cell. Derrick can you get a ride back on campus?" asks Harrison because Derrick rode with him.

"Yeah man, I'll catch you later," says Derrick.

Harrison turns back around to face Toni, Greg and Bahari.

"What time does the movie start," says Bahari.

"I don't know I thought that you were going to find that out," says Harrison as he finishes up the last of Bahari's chicken and lo mein noodles.

Harrison closes the empty food container.

"Was my food good?" asks Bahari with a slight smile.

"Yes, thanks babe," says Harrison as he reaches over and gives Bahari a kiss.

"Sometimes you can be so greedy," says Bahari softly as she kisses him again then she reaches for a napkin to wipe his mouth.

"The movie starts in an hour," says Toni, she looked up the show times for the movie on her Iphone.

"Are you done with your food Toni?" asks Greg.

"Yes," says Toni as she closes the empty container.

"I'll take it for you," says Greg as he stands and takes both empty containers to the trash in the food court.

"Before we leave the mall I need to go to get me a pair of shoes," informs Harrison.

"Cool let's go," says Bahari.

The three of them stand as Greg is walking over to them.

"We are going to Footlocker downstairs," says Toni.

"Cool," says Greg and he offers to carry Toni's bags.

Toni is a little surprised she did not know that Greg was so chivalrous, but she was relieved. It was nice to be with a man that was considerate and had good manners which is something she has found hard to find in her age group.She had heard of sisters that say white men treat you better by their assumption, most of them are raised in two parent homes and that they would never date a brother again. She had never looked at a white boy, sure she had seen a few she thought was cute, but she just never gave it a second thought.

After leaving Footlocker the foursome went to the movie and then to a party, but Harrison and Bahari did not stay long, they wanted to be alone so Greg made sure that Toni got back to the dorms safely after the party.

Bahari and Harrison went to a park for a late night stroll; the weather was a cool sixty five degrees, but better than what the weather is at this time of year in Chicago. They both had on their jackets and gloves and if worse turns to worse they will have each other's body heat to keep them warm.

The park is well lit on the weekends until twelve o'clock midnight. The park was sprinkled with big old oak trees and it had a jogging path, it was a great night for a scroll there were a few other couples walking and talking as they were, some of the couples were wrapped up in blankets and there was a nice light coming from the full moon that cast a kind of grayish blue light on the park itself.

"Harrison where do you see yourself after college," asks Bahari as she squeezes Harrison's hand.

"Well I hope to be playing in the NBA, have a bachelor's degree and hopefully you will be wearing my ring," says Harrison as he wraps his arm around her tighter.

"Do you still want three and a half children?" asks Bahari with a smile.

"Yes, I do. I don't want my kids to be lonely like I was growing up I want them to have each other," says Harrison in a serious tone.

"Me either, I always wanted a sister, but my parents said they always wanted just one kid because of their careers," says Bahari as she wraps her other arm around Harrison's back.

"You sure about that because being a Doctor is a demanding career you sure you are going to want to come home and change diapers," says Harrison jokingly.

"Yes, I can't wait to be a mother to our children," says Bahari.

They stop walking and Harrison plants a passionate kiss on her.

"You and I are going to have a nice future together, I love you," says Harrison as they kiss again passionately.

"We need to stop this because sometimes when we kiss I get a funny feeling in my stomach and I want to do more, as in make love to you," says Bahari as she looks up at him.

"Me too I want to wait, but sometimes I want you so bad that I cannot sleep at night," adds Harrison as he stares down at her.

"I know the first time is going to be beautiful we just have to be strong," says Bahari as she hugs him.

Harrison reaches down and kisses the top of her head as they stand and hold each other before they commence to walking again.

"I want two boys and a girl," says Bahari with a smile.

"I want all boys, girls are too much trouble," says Harrison.

"I just want one, but whatever God decides to bless us with will be fine with me," says Bahari.

"Me too, as long as they are happy and we are all together, I'm good," says Harrison as he scoops her up and carries her.

Bahari is laughing as he runs through the park acting as if he is going to drop her.

"Put me down," says Bahari laughing so hard she can hardly catch her breath.

Finally Harrison stops running and places her on the ground; he hovers over her then she lays back. Harrison gets on top of her and they kiss passionately again.

"I always want us to be together," says Harrison.

"Me too, I love you," says Bahari as she stares Harrison in the eyes.

"I love you too, but let's go before that something happens that we don't want to," says Harrison as he gets off of her then helps her up.

Bahari brushes herself off and the two hold hands as they began to walk back to their cars.

"Are we going to church tomorrow?" asks Bahari as she is sitting in her car, letting it warm up before she drives off. Harrison is standing on the outside.

"Yes, I'll come pick you up at ten, put your seatbelt on," says Harrison as he reaches in and gives her a kiss.

"Okay I'll be ready," says Bahari.

"Call me when you get back to the dorms so that I know you got back okay," says Harrison as he softly hits the top of the car.

"I will, love you, bye," says Bahari as she blows a kiss at Harrison.

"I love you too, be safe," says Harrison.

Bahari drives slowly until she sees that Harrison has made it into his car then she drives off,while thinking to herself how much she loves him.

Harrison drives away from the park thinking how lucky he is to have met such a smart, beautiful woman that loves him and really knows him. He thought about all the women he has met while at Duke and they are interested in him because he is a ball player, but Bahari is different she has known him his whole life. His friends have asked him, "How do you know you love her if you have never had anything or anyone to compare her to." His explanation is, "I don't need a comparison,Bahari is what I want."

Chapter Four

It is April and the basketball season is over and Harrison has decided to enter his name into The 2013 NBA Draft with the support of his family, teammates, fans and the coaching staff at Duke.

Harrison finished the year with a winning season and he just turned nineteen a month ago.

Harrison and his Sports Agent Antonio Martin made their announcement after talking it over with his family and coaches because you cannot return to college after you have hired an agent due to loss of amateur status. Mr. Martin had set up interviews and workouts with NBA teams and Harrison had attended a pre-draft camp in Orlando Florida, all of his hard work as well as his taking lessons on how to deal with the media came out favorable. Theadministration and the students are a buzz as the news catches fire on ESPN, CNN, the local news channels and everywhere else across the country that sports is broadcast.

Harrison along with family (some whom flew in from Trinidad and Barbados for the occasion), friends, some of his Duke Teammates and coaches are at his home a few weeks later to watch the draft on television together.

Harrison's home is decorated in red, white and blue for the Los Angeles Clippers, the team that Harrison so desperately wants to be drafted to. He has a beautiful cake that is designed to look like the Clipper stadium. Harrison and his family have on the Clipper's jerseys and so does Bahari and her parents.

Harrison's Grandmother has made all of his favorites; curry oxtails, greens, cornbread, curry chicken, callaloo, crab n' dumpling, cabbage, okra and tomatoes, pigeon peas and rice. His dad and uncle got a snow cone machine and she made shaved ice, a favorite from when he was a child.

"Are you excited?" asked Greg.

"Yes, but you guys had better take the championship next season or I'm coming back and kick some butt," says Harrison with a smile.

"Hey we gone miss you man," says Harry another teammate from Duke.

"I'm going to miss you guys too, but you will see me on television slamming and dunking on them guys," says Harrison as he mashes Harry on the top of his head as he passes him to take a seat next to him.

All of a sudden they hear the clanging of his mother hitting the side of a champagne glass with a fork.

"Settle down everyone Harrison's father and I have an announcement to make," says Katina Allen.

"Please make sure all of our guests have a drink so that we may make a toast," says Mr. Allen to the servers.

"Sure," says one of the servers with a smile on her face.

After a few minutes the Allen's began their toast.

"Today is a proud day for the Allen family, our son Harrison will be leaving to play in the NBA in the morning and we are so excited for him, he has made us proud. We wish you health, strength and endurance on your road to the NBA and me and your mom free tickets," says Mr. Allen as the crowd burst into laughter.

"Dad," says Harrison with a smile.

"Sincerely son we are proud of you and we wish you well," says Mr. Allen as he raises his glass and taps other guests and family glasses as well as his wife's before he gives her a kiss and takes a sip.

"Harrison, you are my baby, you grew up so fast it seems like yesterday you were bouncing that basketball all the time and getting on my nerves. You always said you wanted to play in the NBA and today your dreams have come true. I am going to be the proudest Mom when they announce your name today. I will miss you son," says Mrs. Allen with tears welling up in her eyes.

Harrison walks over and gives his mother a hug and a kiss.

"Mom I am not leaving you, I promise to call frequently and visit as much as my schedule will allow," says Harrison in a sincere tone.

Harrison hugs his dad.

"I have an announcement of my own," says Harrison.

"Come here Bahari," says Harrison as he holds his hand out for Bahari to come and stand next to him.

"I have the best parents, friends and family that anyone could ask for and for that I am grateful. I have also had the privilege of being in love with the same girl since I was a little boy (the guest laughs) the next time that we are gather again whether it is here on in Los Angeles it will be for my wedding to this beautiful woman standing next to me. I love you, Bahari and I thank you all for being here for me today," says Harrison as he kisses Bahari and takes a drink of his apple cider.

The crowd cheers and they all take a sip of their drinks.

"I love you too, Harrison," says Bahari as she kisses Harrison on the lips again.

The crowd hears clanging again, but this time it is coming from Bahari's father, Kenneth Johnson.

"I have something to say (pause). I have known this young man all his life and he is smart, respectable and talented on the basketball court. He has been like a son to me and my wife, Bethany and I am sure he will make us proud to one day officially call him son, we wish you well," said Mr. Johnson as he raises his glass in the air. Harrison shakes his hand then the two men hug, Mrs. Johnson has a big smile on her face.

"I am so proud of Harrison, but I am mad with him all at the same time because I have to go back to Duke University without my best friend, I will miss you," says Bahari sadly as she raises her glass with tears in her eyes.

Harrison gives her a hug and a kiss.

Later when Harrison's name was called for the L.A. Clippers choice in the first round there is a thunderous cheer, clapping, high-fives and a few tears were shed by Harrison, guest and family members.

Harrison's coach from Duke, Coach Dickerson asked that the members of the team that were present to sing the Duke Fight song, "Blue and White."

After the fight song and a few more toast from family, friends, coaches and teammates the party switches into overdrive with a dance contest and karaoke, around two a.m. the party comes to an end.

When Harrison is preparing to get into bed he hears a knock on the door.

"Come in," says Harrison as he pulls the sheets back on his bed.

"Hi, Son," says Katina.

"Hi," says Harrison dryly as he takes a seat on the side of the bed.

His mother takes a seat beside him.

"What's the matter son?"

"I won't be living here anymore and this won't be my room anymore."

"Honey, this will always be your home no matter what."

There is a knock at the door.

"What's going on in here," says Gwenn, Harrison's grandmother.

"Nothing Grandma, just talking," says Harrison.

"Don't worry it's just nerves and when you come home to visit your room will be the same as when you left it, okay," says Katina as she reaches over and gives her son a kiss on the cheek.

"Let me have a word with him alone," asks Grandma Gwenn.

"Okay, I'll be going to bed now," says Katina with a smile as she gets off the bed and walks out of the bedroom.

Gwenn sits down on the side of the where just a few moments ago Harrison's mother had sat. "Son you know grandma loves you so much and you are about to go off to the big city and play ball. Son I want you to remember what is important; God and family," says Gwenn in her thick island voice.

Harrison looks at her and hugs her tight.

"I won't forget Grandma; can you come back if I send you a ticket to see my first game?"

"I sure will, where else would I be."

"So, you tinking boutmarrying, Bahari?"

"Yes, one day."

"Well I'm glad she is smart, cute and you know she ain't after your money."

Harrison agrees because he knows his grandmother is known for speaking her mind.

"Cause boy dem girls gone be after you especially dem white ones, you ain't never brought no white woman home and don't you start."

Harrison says nothing he just smiles. Grandma Gwenn can speak her mind at times and she thinks that all white people have an agenda.

"You know what I say, If she can't use a comb don't brang her home," says Gwenn and the two of them burst into laughter.

Gwenn gets off the bed and kisses Harrison on the cheek.

"I love you."

"I love you too, Grandma."

Chapter Five

Harrison has been in Los Angeles for two weeks and some of the players have invited him to a nightclub.

When they arrive at the club they drive up to the valet; Terry, 7-series BMW, Terrance, Porsche and Chris has a Black Hummer. They all meet at the door of the club all four men are looking good, draped in platinum, diamonds and smelling good.

The bouncer at the door a muscle bound dark skinned brother recognized Chris, the forward for the L.A. Clippers on the team and immediately he removed the red velvet rope and let them through. When we walked into The Apple nightclub it was a buzz with a mixed ethnicity of party-goers and the DJ was playing a Lil Wayne hit.

We were immediately ushered to the VIP section where Chris gave his AMEX card to the hostess to start a tab.

"Can you bring us some Hennessy XO please and some Dom Perignon Champagne for the ladies," says Chris.

"This place is huge," says Harrison.

"I come here every so often, the place is always packed with beautiful woman," says Terrance.

"Hey, I think I see my girl Tammy, I am going to go and say Hi, maybe she let a brother get lucky," says Terry.

Terry walks out of the VIP section.

Harrison sees him talking to a beautiful woman across the room. She has a white dress on that dips low in the back, plunging neckline and very short, but she is stunning to look at, she is black, tall with almond shaped eyes with a short Halle Berry cut.

The DJ makes a shout out, "Hey everybody my homeboy Chris of the L.A. Clippers is in the club along with teammates Terrance and Terry. I see ya kid; ladies make your way to the VIP and make my boy feel welcome. Pretty girls only please."

The DJ then plays, "All I do is win" by DJ Khalid and the crowd goes into overdrive. The two security guards that were guarding the VIP section moved the velvet rope and selected a few of the female party-goers to let into VIP, before long the section was filled with women, with some of them fighting for Chris' and Terrance's attention. Some of the ladies hurried to sit on either side of Terrance and Chris and the others that were not lucky to get a seat next to them sat on the white velvet couch and some of them stood. They were all given a glass of Dom Perignon and Chris did a toast.

"To my new teammate Harrison, welcome to Los Angeles the land of opportunity, prosperity and beautiful women," said Chris.

They all take sips of their drinks.

"Okay let's party," said Terrance.

Chris and Terrance take the hands of two women each and head to the dance floor.

"Hi, how are you," says one of the ladies.

"Hi, I'm good how are you?"

"I'm Diane, so you are new to the team?"

"Yes, I am."

"Have you ever been to Los Angeles before?"

"I've been to L.A. once when I was fourteen with my parents."

"What position do you play?"

"Point Guard."

"So you think you can stop me from scoring?"

"Huh, yes I think so," says Harrison with a smile. He was taken aback by her candor.

After a few minutes of small talk he asks Diane which way was the restroom then he excuses himself.

On his return from the restroom he sees a strikingly beautiful young lady standing alone gyrating to the sounds of the beat coming from the enormous speakers strategically placed around the club.

Her beauty stops him in his tracks. She has golden brown skin, long thick naturally curly hair, petite, yet very curvy in the hips and the straightest whitest teeth he has ever seen. She has on black shorts, a blue and white halter top with her back and mid-drift out, a pair of strappy sandals that are decorated with black and blue stones that look like diamonds. She looks to be of Puerto Rican descent.

Harrison walks over to the woman.

"Hi," says Harrison as he extends his hand.

"Hi," says the woman.

"My name is Harrison and I saw you standing here alone, are you with someone?" asked Harrison.

"My girlfriend, but I haven't seen her in awhile," says the woman looking a little annoyed.

"What's your name?" asked Harrison.

"Chutney."

"Hi, Chutney, would you like to dance?"

Chutney looks around the club then she accepts his offer.

Harrison extends his arm with a smile and escorts her onto the floor.

They dance, but she is showing him up with her moves on the dance floor.

After three songs Harrison asks her back to VIP and she accepts.

When Diane sees Harrison coming back to VIP with another girl she shoots him a nasty look she fills her glass up with some champagne and she sits down with an annoyed look on her face.

Harrison notices the nasty stares, but he says nothing and he and Chutney take a seat.

"Would you like a glass of champagne?" asks Harrison.

"Sure," says Chutney.

Harrison scoots to the edge of his seat grabs a clean champagne flute and pours her a glass and hands the glass to her.

Harrison sits back in his seat he notices Chutney's beautiful long legs and her beautiful white smile.

"So are you from L.A.?"

"No, I moved here."

"Are you?"

"No, I am from Tennessee, I'm a model."

"Oh, I see, you are beautiful, where has your picture appeared maybe I've seen you before."

"I've done some work for J. C. Penney for their Christmas catalog, an ad in a gentlemen's magazine modeling underwear and I've done some work for the House of Dereon, a jean ad in Jet magazine."

Harrison begins to clap, Chutney tries to put his hands down because his clapping is drawing attention to her they both smile.

"I'm impressed."

"That's nothing I want to do some major modeling like my friend I came here with tonight, I am struggling just to get jobs, but she looks out for me though."

"That's great as long as you are doing something you love, it will happen for you."

"I hope so."

Terry returns to VIP with the beautiful woman on his arm that he saw him talking to earlier.

"I see you are making friends," says Terry.

"Yeah, this is my new friend Chutney," says Harrison.

"Harrison this is Tammy, my old friend," says Terry with a smile.

Tammy hits him in his bicep.

"Hello," says Tammy as she extends her hand for Harrison to shake it.

"Tammy where have you been?" asks Chutney.

"With Terry on the dance floor, at the bar in the Hookah Lounge," says Tammy as she looks at Terry with a sly grin.

"You two know each other?" asks Harrison.

"Yes, this is the friend that I came here with," says Chutney.

"Oh," says Harrison.

"Baby, can I have a glass of champagne?" asks Tammy.

"Sure, you can have whatever you like," says Terry in the tone like how T.I's song says.

Terry reaches over and kisses her on the cheek.

"Where is Chris and Terrance?" asks Harrison.

"I saw Terrance a few minutes ago with his on again off again flame, Rosalyn. I don't know why he won't just marry her. Chris, I left him at the bar entertaining two ladies," says Terry.

Tammy takes a sip of her wine then she excuses herself to go to the restroom to freshen up her makeup.

"Come with me Chutney," says Tammy as she is pulling on Chutney to stand up.

"I'll be right back," says Chutney with a smile as she sits her drink down to go to the ladies room.

"We will be right here," says Terry as the two men watch the women walk away.

"Chutney is gorgeous and she seems to be sweet. Tammy is cute too," says Harrison.

"She is, take my word for it," says Terry as he takes a sip of his Hennessy and coke.

"Man, must you be so foul," says Harrison.

"Hey, let a dog be a dog," says Terry as he starts to howl as if he is looking at the moon.

They both burst into laughter.

Diane comes over and takes a seat beside Harrison.

"You know we can still hook up later after the club," says Diane in Harrison's ear.

"I don't think so, but it was nice to meet you though, are you enjoying yourself?" asks Harrison.

Diane doesn't say a word she gives him a dirty look sits her champagne glass down on the table in front of him and leaves the VIP area.

"Man what did you say to her?" asks Terry.

They both see Chris coming back to VIP with only one of the girls he left with and a new girl.

"I don't like women that are so forward, she literally wanted to take my clothes off right here," says Harrison in an annoyed tone.

"And what is wrong with that?" asks Terry with a smile.

"I don't like it, I like subtle women," says Harrison.

"They all want the same thing."

(Meanwhile In the restroom)

Chutney and Tammy are in the mirror at the club putting on a fresh layer of makeup.

"How did you meet Harrison, you know he is the new star Point Guard for the Clippers," says Tammy as she is applying her lipstick.

"No I didn't know that," says Chutney.

"He just signed a contract witha 2 million dollar sign-on bonus and 12 million dollars over 4 years and that does not include his endorsements. He was the first round draft pick for the L.A. Clippers. Terry plays for them also, you've heard me talk about him you just never met him that's all," says Tammy admiring herself in the mirror.

"So he has a lot of money, huh?"

"Alot of it."

"He seems to be nice, just freakishly tall and I generally go for the light-skinned model types."

"I know, but it may be time for a change. I can tell he likes you at least get a real date out of it or maybe a new pair of designer shoes. Terry has bought me several pair, hell he bought the shoes I got on right now."

Chutney looks down at Tammy's shoes though she noticed them earlier she wanted to get another look and as usual I am sure they are designer shoes because of the red bottoms, probably a gift. Tammy has always had men buying her things. Since I met her a year ago and though she is not a high dollar model she does well financially for herself. Her one- bedroom loft apartment is decorated to the nines and she wears nothing but name brand clothes, shoes and purses. Actually, the halter Chutney is wearing belongs to Tammy.

Chutney has been sleeping in Tammy's guest bedroom slash loft for the past eight months but, Tammy doesn't mind because she is hardly there, besides she has someone to take care of her apartment in her absence.

Modeling jobs for Chutney have been sporadic and if it had it not been for meeting Tammy and her generosity she would be on the streets. Living in L.A. is very expensive, especially for a struggling young model.

Chutney left home a week after graduation with the money she was given as gifts for graduation and savings from working at Star Bucks. She came to L.A. to make it as amodel, unfortunately with the cost of living in L.A. that money was gone in six months. Though the waitress job pays it's just not enough for the lifestyle that she so desperately wants.

"You keep saying you want to see a Clipper's game, well maybe now you will get your chance."

"Maybe I will, but he had better be really nice because he is taking me out of my comfort zone."

"Girl you ain't got a comfort zone, you are broke. You can't sleep in my loft forever."

"I know I just need a break."

"Well he might be that break."

"How long have you known Terry?"

"I met him last season we had a little one-night stand and tonight is looking like we gone be having another that brother knows what to do with some poo-nanny."

"I hear you."

The two slap hands while giggling.

After they both apply a little more makeup they exit the ladies room and join the guys in VIP.

Chris comes and sits down by Harrison and the ladies.

"I am ready to go and hit some skins," says Chris as he waves to the two ladies at the other end of the white suede couch. They wave back while smiling.

Terrance returns to the VIP with Rosalyn in tow.

"Hello everyone," says Rosalyn with a smile as she shakes Tammy and Chutney's hand.

"Hello," said both women in unison.

"I am about to get outta here, it's late and I got two ladies that are going to model some skin for me, if you know what I mean," says Chris.

"Me too, I just came over to say goodnight, had a good time and I'll holla," says Terrance.

"Tammy you going with me or am I going with you?" asks Terry.

"I am going with you because I got my girl with me. I am going to let her take my car. Take care of my baby," informs Tammy as she hands Chutney her keys.

"I will, have a good time," says Chutney as she stands to leave.

Chris waves the waitress over to settle his tab and afterwards they all exit the VIP.

"Can I walk you to your car?" asks Harrison.

"Sure," says Chutney.

"Call me as soon as you get home," says Tammy as she is getting into Terry's car.

"I will," says Chutney as she waves to her.

"I would like to call and make sure you got home safely too."

"Are you asking me for my number?"

"I am."

"You got your phone?'

Yes, right here," as Harrison pulls it out of his pocket.

"310-718-????"

"I got it, you are officially locked in."

"We are here and thanks for walking me to the car."

Harrison takes the keys from her, unlocks the doors and watches her get safely inside Tammy's red C-Class Mercedes.

Chutney rolls down the window when he shuts the door.

"It was nice meeting you."

"It was nice meeting you too."

"I am going to take you up on your offer to show me around L.A."

"Okay, well you know the number."

"Okay, call you in about an hour."

"Okay."

"Drive safely."

"I will," says Chutney and she drives away.

Harrison walks back to the entrance of the club so the he can get his car from valet.

When he arrives back at his condominium he takes a shower and as he is drying off, his cell phone rings and its Bahari.

"Hello."

"Hi baby did you have a good time with the fellas?"

"Yes, the clubs out here are huge."

"You didn't drink too much did you?"

"No dear, just some champagne and a shot of Hennessy."

"I'm just worried about you driving," says Bahari.

"How was your day and why are you not asleep it is three a.m.?"

"I wanted to talk to you before I went to bed, is that okay?"

"Yes, but I am exhausted. I am about to hit the sack and you should too."

"I love you."

"I love you too, call me tomorrow. Are you going to church?"

"Yes, are you?"

"Maybe, I have got to find a church out here. I am still looking."

"Call me when you get out of church."

"Harrison, are you okay?"

"Yes, I'm just tired."

"Okay, get some sleep. Love you."

"I love you too, bye."

"Bye Babe."

When Harrison hangs up the phone he puts on his pajamas, gets bottled water from the fridge then gets in bed. He looks at Chutney's number then he decides to call her.

The phone rings once and she answers.

"Hello."

"Did I wake you?"

"Yeah, I was drifting off a little. I didn't think you were going to call."

"I said I would."

"All the doors and windows locked."

"Yes, they are."

"It was really nice meeting you tonight, when can I see you again?"

"Not sure, when would you like to."

"Tomorrow, can I take you to brunch?"

"Yes, where?"

"Well you tell me, I'm new here wherever you want to go."

"Okay, I will take you to one of my favorite spots in the valley."

"What is it?"

"It's called the Blu Jam Café and the Crunchy French toast is the best I have ever tasted."

"Are we meeting there or can I come and pick you up because that's what I'd prefer."

"Yes, come at ten o'clock and I'll be ready."

"Send me your address."

"I will as soon as we hang up."

"I am about to let you go because If you want me up and at your house by ten I need some sleep little lady."

"Okay, see you in the morning."

"Okay, goodnight."

"Goodnight."

After Harrison hangs up the phone he feels funny about making a breakfast date with her as far as Bahari was concerned, but he has not done anything wrong. It is a harmless breakfast, but with a beautiful woman.

Harrison turns over and puts the phone on the charger then he turns out the light until he drifts to sleep.

Chapter Six

Harrison and Chutney are shown to their seats at the Blu Jam Café and they are handed menus.

"So this place is a favorite of yours?"

"Yes, Tammy took me here for brunch when we first met and I was hooked."

"What do you recommend?"

"The French toast, it's a large helping, but it is so good."

"Okay French toast it is."

The waiter comes and takes their orders they both order the French toast and milk.

"Do you miss your family, Chutney?"

"Sometimes, I haven't been for a visit since a left almost a year ago."

"Why is that?"

"My money is funny if you know what I mean."

"Yeah, I do."

The waiter comes and brings them their milk and assures them that their order is coming soon.

"Do you miss yours?"

"Yeah, like today it's Sunday and I know my Mom has made a big breakfast then we would all go to church together then she would make Sunday dinner, yummy."

"So you guys are close, huh."

"Yes we are. Are you close to your family?"

"Not really, my father has never been around or supported me and my mother she is working all the time. She has two jobs and I was always stuck watching Savaughn, my four year old nephew, a six year old brother, Reshawn and my thirteen year old sister, Michelle."

"Oh, so you are the oldest of three."

"No, I have a sister, but she is on drugs and my mother is raising her son."

"Oh."

"But it's okay. I am going to become famous and take care of my mother so she does not have to work so hard, she never went to college so she has always been a maid and a cook all my life. She needs a break and that's why I can't go back home broke I got to make it out here one way or another. I send her money when I can."

"That's very noble of you that you want to help your mother."

"I know your mother is proud of you because you play basketball and all."

"Yes, she is, but my parents are pretty well off they are both doctors."

"So you are a rich kid?"

"Yes, but I worked hard for a position on the team unfortunately you can't buy that."

The waiter comes back and places their food in front of them.

Harrison reaches for her hand and graces the food.

Chutney is a little embarrassed because she forgot and was reaching for her fork so that she may start to eat the French toast that smelled so good on the plate in front of her smothered in strawberries and whipped cream.

"You got time after we eat to take me to the mall I want to pick up something."

"Sure, do you have a girlfriend back home? Where did you say you were from?"

"I am from Chicago. Yes, I am seeing someone she and I have known each other from childhood."

"What would she say if she knew you were having brunch with me?"

"She would be a little upset. Honestly Chutney this is the first time another woman has peaked my curiosity, maybe I'm just lonely."

"Really, do you miss her?"

"Yes I do. She attends Duke University and she will be coming out here for a visit in two weeks."

"Are you guys serious?"

"Yes, we intend to marry when she finishes her doctorates degree."

"Well that is serious."

"I am attracted to you (sigh) I can't believe I just said that."

"Well thanks for your honesty and besides we have not broken any rules. Let's just enjoy our brunch and be two friends enjoying each other's company."

"Okay, I'd like that."

They have small talk and finish their meals and head to The Beverly Center Mall.

They go to stores such as Just Cavalli, Bloomingdale's, Macy's for Men and Banana Republic.

As they are passing Louis Vuitton Harrison notices that Chutney is staring at a pair of patent leather shoes in the window.

"Hey, let's go in and look around."

"Sure."

"Hello is there anything I can help you with today?" asks the Italian looking salesman.

"Yes, I think she would like to see those black patent leather shoes in the window."

"Harrison I can't afford those I was just looking at them."

"They are on sale today."

"I still can't afford them."

"They are free."

"Nothing in here is free."

"Today it is for you."

"Now tell the man what size you wear."

Chutney smiles at Harrison and quickly turns to the salesman and says, "I'll take a size six."

"I'll be right back," says the salesman with a smile on his face.

"You don't have to do this, they cost nine hundred dollars and besides we just met."

"I know, I want to and I am sure they will be cute on you."

The salesman returns with the shoe and takes them out of the box for her.

When Chutney puts the shoes on her feet she stands to look in the mirror to admire them on her feet.

"Do you like them? Are they comfortable?" asks Harrison.

"They are, but do you like them?"

"I do, but it's not about me liking them, do you like them?" asks Harrison.

"Yes," says Chutney with a smile.

"We will take them, thank you," says Harrison to the salesman.

The salesman nods his head with a smile.

"Thank you," squeals Chutney as she is taking the shoes off and places them back in the box.

"You're welcome," says Harrison with a smile.

"It's the least I can do since I have taken up your time on a Sunday afternoon," says Harrison.

After they purchase the shoes they visit a few more stores then head back to the parking garage.

"Thanks for your time today."

"Oh, you are welcome and thanks for the shoes, I love them they are my first pair of designer shoes."

"Not a problem. When can I see you again?"

"Do you think that is wise since you have a girlfriend?"

"We are just friends and as you said earlier we have not broken any laws."

"True. Well how about dinner a girls gotta eat and Tammy has to leave for a shoot in Arizona tonight so I will be alone."

"Okay, what time?"

"Say about seven?"

"Sounds good to me, I will see you then."

Harrison pulls up to where Chutney lives and gets out the car to open the door for her.

She grabs her bag with the shoes in it.

"See you soon."

"Okay, but can you wear those shoes for me?"

"Did you think I wasn't?" says Chutney with a smile as she walks away and up the stairs.

Harrison gets into his car and drives away.

As Harrison is walking into his Condo his cell phone rings and it is Bahari.

"Hello."

"Hey you, what are you up to today?"

"Just got back from the mall I was just going to watch a little television and chill for awhile."

"You miss me?"

"Of course I do."

"Do you miss me?"

"Yes, all the time. I can't wait to see you."

"Me too, how is Toni?"

"She's fine, getting on my nerves as usual."

"How do you think that our relationship is going to work out with you being on the east coast and me on the west?"

"Well baby we love each other so we will make it work, why?"

"It's just that I am out here alone and I miss you."

"I miss you too and besides we talked about this."

"Have you ever thought about dating other people Bahari and you can be honest with me."

"No, what are you saying Harrison?"

"Nothing maybe because it is Sunday and I just miss you and my folks. It has been a month since I saw a familiar face is all."

"You sure that's all it is?"

"Yes, Bahari, don't go reading anything else into it. So what do you have planned for your day?"

"I don't know just some shopping and studying I may even take in a movie."

"That would be nice. Later I am going to go and grab something to eat, but other than that I am just going to stay in and let the television entertain me."

"Baby these next few days are going to fly by and then I will be there to cook, clean and take care of you, okay."

"Okay."

"Don't sound so sad, I'll be there for a whole week and you can show me around the city."

"Okay I got to get some things lined up for us to do."

"Not looking for a lot to do I am coming to spend some alone time with you, that's good enough for me."

"Okay, but this separation is killing me."

"I know me too, but we both have our careers and we have got to stay focused just a few more years and we will be married."

"You sure you still want to marry me?"

"Yes, that is the one thing in my life that I am sure of."

"I will call you later, take care."

"You too, I love you."

"I love you too."

They both hang up the phone.

Bahari is a little worried about some of the things Harrison said in reference to them dating other people.

Harrison is a little bothered by his attraction to Chutney, but he can't wait to see her again tonight, he keeps telling himself, "I have NOT broken any rules."

Harrison decides to take a nap.

(Later that evening)

At seven o'clock sharp Harrison is pulling up to Chutney's residence. He parks the car and walks up to the door and rings the bell.

Chutney opens the door.

"Hey, I am almost dressed, come in and have a seat."

"Just like a woman, never on time."

"Well I was trying to be extra cute especially since I was wearing my new shoes."

"Oh, that's why you are late, huh?"

"Make yourself comfortable I will be out in a minute."

Harrison takes a seat and looks around the apartment.

It is a modest apartment decorated with a Spanish flare. The couch and loveseat are a burnt orange color with blue and brown pillows, a large screen television hangs on the wall, the floors are a dark mahogany wood, the kitchen appliances are stainless steel with a center island and the walls are decorated with pictures of Tammy. The coffee table has a large bouquet of flowers on it that has flowers with the colors of blue, orange, brown and yellow with a slight bit of green.

"How many bedrooms are in here?"

"One, but it has a loft, which is where I sleep."

"Why?"

"I was just asking this is very nice."

"Thanks, I'll be sure to tell Tammy you said so."

"How long have you been living with Tammy?"
"About seven or eight months."

In walks Chutney into the living room.

"I'm ready."

Harrison stands to his feet.

"Yes, you are. You look beautiful and you smell good too."

"Thank you, you look nice too."

Chutney has on a red baby doll dress, her hair flat ironed and raked over to one side and her makeup is done to perfection. Her new shoes really look good with the dress.

Harrison has on an Armani fitted yellow and white striped button down shirt, blue jeans and a pair of Michael Kors brown dress shoes.

Harrison holds out his arm, she wraps her arm around his and they head out the door.

When they arrive at the Palm Restaurant it is a little crowded, but luckily Harrison was told by a teammate that it would be best if they made a reservation for that reason, so that the wait wouldn't be too long.

They feasted on jumbo lump crabmeat crab cakes, baked clams casino, prime bone-in rib eye steaks, and filet mignon and for dessert big iced carrot cake that was so big neither of them could finish it so they asked to take it home.

"It's still early and unless you are ready to go home I would love to go somewhere else."

"Like where?"

"You tell me?"

"Let's go to L.A. Live they got movies, bowling and bars. Want to have some drinks then catch a movie?"

"Sure let's do it."

When they arrive at L.A. Live they check the theater to see what was playing then they went to a bar where Harrison had a beer and Chutney had a martini.

They never made it to the movie because they got so engaged in conversation at the bar that they missed the movie, but neither of them cared they were enjoying each other's company.

Around 1 a.m. they left L.A. Live and headed home.

Harrison got out of the car to open her door for her.

"I had a great time, Chutney."

"I did too."

"Do you date much?"

"No, not really, I am just trying to stay focused on my almost non-existent modeling career."

"Don't say that you will be fine things are just slow right now."

"If things don't start to happen soon I am going to have to go back home, broke."

"You won't be broke, we all are trying to get somewhere in our careers."

"You are doing fine; you just signed a fat contract."

"Yes, but if I don't perform my behind will not be in a Clippers uniform for long."

Chutney just stares at him.

"As fine as you are stop feeling sorry for yourself and sell yourself, get out there and pound the pavement."

"That's easy to say when you have a car."

"Tammy is gone right now you have access to her car, girl get on your grind."

"I do, but I don't have the expensive headshots they want. I need a really good photographer there are plenty in L.A. but a lot of them are scandalous they try to get you to pose nude."

"Really, well have you thought of getting a job until you hit the big time?"

"Yes, I waitress at a bar the tips are really good, but after I pay Tammy, buy food, pay cab and bus fares there isn't a lot left, but I can just feel it I am going to make it. I am only 21 and I don't have this beautiful skin and these big beautiful hazel eyes for nothing or atleast that's what my grandfather tells me."

"Really, well your grandfather is right he knows a beauty when he sees one."

Chutney smiles and gives Harrison a hug.

"I am going to go in now. Thanks for dinner and the drinks because had it not been for you I would have eaten a sandwich and went to bed early."

"No problem, but keep your head up something is going to happen for you soon."

"Thanks Harrison, have a good night."

Chutney waves goodbye and walks toward her front door.

"Bye Chutney."

Harrison gets into his car when he sees her open the door and walk in he drives away.

"I really like this girl," Harrison says to himself.

Harrison reaches into his glove compartment and turns his cell phone back on and he sees where he has missed three calls Bahari and three text messages:

"Are you okay, I keep calling and your phone is going straight to voicemail, call me."

"Where are you I am beginning to get worried, call me?"

"Harrison, what is going on please call me I don't care how late it is, call me."

82

"Crap what am I going to say to her," says Harrison aloud.

His cell phone rings and it is Bahari.

Harrison answers, yet tries to sound happy to hear from her and he was, just not right now he needed more time to figure out what he was going to say to her.

"Hi Baby."

"Hey, where are you? I have been calling and texting and your phone kept going to voicemail," says Bahari in an angry tone.

"Babe I was out having dinner then I went to a bar and lost track of time."

"That's fine, but what was wrong with your phone?"

"It died so I left it in the car."

Harrison has a funny feeling in his stomach because he just lied to Bahari, but he knew telling her the truth was not going to be easy.

"Oh, but are you okay?" asks Bahari in a concerned voice.

"Yes baby, my phone just died, I didn't. Stop making a big deal about it."

"Sounds like you are in your car."

"I am. I am headed home."

"Okay, well I was just worried about you so now that I know you are okay I can go to bed. I was about to call your parents and see if they had heard from you."

"Bahari don't ever do that and get my parents all upset over nothing."

"I didn't, but I was worried."

"Don't ever do that, I am a grown man and I can handle myself. Look let me let you go so you can get some sleep, I will call you tomorrow."

"Are you angry with me because I don't like the tone in your voice?"

"Babe I am fine just tired (sigh)."

"Okay."

"Goodnight."

"I love you."

"Okay," says Harrison as he quickly hangs up the phone.

Bahari clicks the end button on her cell."What is he going through, I need to go see him," says Bahari to herself she is starting to feel some type of way.

Chapter Seven

Bahari has arrived in L.A., but Harrison is at practice he sent a car for her and the doorman has instructions to let her into his condominium.

When Bahari opens the door she is impressed by the décor of the three bedroom condominium; an open floorplan,the floors are a dark hardwood, white leather couch and loveseat with dark chocolate satin pillows on them, recess lighting throughout, fireplace, dark wood coffee table with a large bouquet of fresh flowers on it with a zebra print throw rug underneath and African accents on the walls.

Exposed dark wood beams on the partially glass ceiling. The kitchen has all stainless steel appliances a center island and a large glass dinner table sitting on a slab of oak wood for six with high backed dark chocolate leather chairs.

Bahari sits her bags down at the doorand walks around the condo then she goes downstairs.

As she walks down a hallway and passes a bathroom dressed in a dark purple décor and she passes another room that has been turned into an office complete with a fax, printer and computer that overlook a wooded area. She passes another room that she assumes is a guest room because of the size, she peeks in and sees that the décor is a brown and green and it comes with a full bath.

When Bahari reaches the end of the long hallway she reaches an expansive room that she is sure is a master suite because of its expansive size. It has a view of the city below with a long patio. There is a king size platform bed, that has blue and silver sheets on it with an over load of pillows, a large dark wood armoire and a hidden television at the foot of the bed, two large oval shaped white chairs with a large red and silver throw rug facing a fireplace.

Bahari opens the door leading out to the patio and walks out to take in the view it was beautiful she lifted her sunglasses up and placed them on the top of her head as the afternoon air blew her hair in the wind. She just smiled and felt blessed to be surrounded by God's beauty.

"Hey I see you made it."

"Hey, you!"

Bahari jumps on Harrison and gives him a big kiss.

"I missed you."

"I missed you too. How was your flight?"

"It was good, the air went out on the plane,and it was hot. I wanted to freshen up before you got home."

"Are you hungry?"

"Yes."

"Okay you want to go out or do you want to order in?"

"Hmmmmm let's order in, we can go out tomorrow."

"Okay, well get comfortable what would you like Italian, Brazilian or Chinese?"

"Italian."

"Okay, I'll get the menu."

"I want to take a shower."

"Okay. I'll order the food, anything specific?"

"As long as you order chicken marsala, I'm happy."

"Okay, I really did miss you, you know."

"Good because I missed you more."

Harrison goes and gets her bags and rolls them into the master suite and starts a bath for her.

Harrison calls the Italian restaurant on the corner and orders the food, takes a bottle of chilled wine out of the fridge and goes through some mail that he brought in from the desk downstairs.

Bahari has gotten out of the shower and lathered her body with Jones and Rose Pretty Gardenia Body Milk and puts Pink Sugar pulse point oils on her neck and wrists. Then she puts on a Victoria Secret pink and white boxer pajama set. She takes her ponytail down, brushes her longhair and applies some lip gloss to her lips.

When she goes into the living room Harrison has spread the food out on the table and is pouring them both a glass of wine.

Harrison walks over and pulls out a seat for her at the table.

"Thank you."

"You are welcome I am so glad that you are here I was really missing you," as Harrison kisses the top of her head and then takes a seat beside her at the table.

"The chicken marsala looks and smells good."

"It is I have had it before."

Bahari takes a sip of her wine then Harrison grabs her hand as they say grace.

They both dig into their food. After dinner they both clear the table and sit down in the living room.

"How are you adjusting to the L.A. lifestyle?"

"I like it out here the restaurants are great, the shopping is good and the people are really nice we have some great fans."

"I want you to come out for my first game."

"I'll be there I think my parents are coming also."

"That would be nice."

Harrison reaches over and kisses Bahari on the lips.

"I love you."

"I love you too, can we watch a movie I see you have plenty?"

"Yeah, I have been buying them like crazy because I don't know a lot of people here just yet so I entertain myself with movies."

Bahari gets up to look at his expansive movie collection.

"Let's watch American Gangster, I love that movie."

"I do too."

Bahari pops American Ganster into the DVD player, Harrison goes and gets a blanket and they snuggle together until they both fall asleep.

(A few days later)

Bahari's trip to L.A. is coming to a close. Harrison has taken her to museums, restaurants, shopping, movies and an amusement park.

Harrison's phone rings, but he is in the shower. Bahari walks over to see who it is on the caller ID.

The phone shows someone by the name of Chutney, but she does not answer.

Later when they are driving to go and get dinner, Harrison is out of the car pumping gas his phone rings again with the same name as before.

When Harrison gets back into the car Bahari is quiet.

"You think you might want to go to a movie afterwards?"

"Sure," says Bahari as she stares out of the window.

"What's the matter babe, are you starting to feel down because you are leaving tomorrow?"

"Harrison, who is Chutney?"

"Why do you ask?"

"Because when you were taking a shower earlier she called and she just called again when you were pumping gas just awhile ago."

"She is a friend."

"When did you meet her?"

"I met her when the fellas and I went out one night."

"You didn't tell me you met anyone."

"Bahari she is just a friend I asked her to show me around the city, one of her friends is dating Terrance, remember he came over one night."

"Yes, but you still have not told me why is she calling you?"

"We just had fun that night and she has shown me around the city she is a model and she is cool, that's all."

"Harrison I am starting to feel that you no longer want to be in a relationship, you want to be single so that you are free to do what you want."

"That's not true I just met that girl I don't know if I like her."

"Oh so you are pondering it, huh."

"Bahari look I have loved you since we were kids and I have never even thought of being with another woman, but I don't see anything wrong with having friends of the opposite sex."

Harrison pulls the car over into a parking lot so that they may talk and he didn't want to have such a conversation in the restaurant.

"So you want to have so called friends does that mean I can too."

"I never said you couldn't."

"I know, but out of respect for you I don't especially not the kind that call me at night."

"Bahari we are no longer kids and besides I am allowed to have friends, what are you choosing my friends now?"

"No Harrison, but you are changing and yes I noticed that you got a late night phone call the other night, maybe that was her too."

"Maybe it was."

"Harrison, take me back to the Condo I am no longer hungry."

"Bahari, come on don't be mad. I am not saying that I don't want to be with you anymore I just think that with the separation I don't want you to miss out on anything, I want you to explore your options."

"Is that what you have been doing with Chutney?"

"We just went to brunch."

"Really you didn't tell me that either," says Bahari as tears began to fill her eyes.

"Bahari, I have not broken any rules nor have I touched her."

"But if you continue to spend time with her you will."

"Look I don't want to hurt you in anyway. I just think that was so high school how we had never dated other people and I think that I want to."

"Well I guess I don't have a choice then, huh."

"I don't want you to be mad at me, please let's just go to dinner and enjoy your last night in L.A."

"Harrison that's not going to make me feel better because the truth is my boyfriend wants to date other women."

"Bahari I never said I wanted to break up."

"Harrison, you are saying it just in another way."

"NO, I am not."

"Fine there has been a few guys on campus that want to take me out anyway especially the ones that knew you and I were dating before you went into the NBA."

"Is there anyone that you wanted to have sex with?"

"No, Harrison, how can you say that to me? I wanted to save that for my wedding night with my husband, the man I wanted to marry."

"And you still can, she is just a friend."

"Do you have feelings for her?"

"No, Bahari I just met her."

"But you want to get to know her better, huh."

"Maybe we shouldn't be having this conversation right now, let's go and enjoy our dinner we can talk about it later."

"Fine Harrison," says Bahari as she crosses her arms and stares out the window.

Harrison starts back up the car and they head to the restaurant. At the restaurant there is very little conversation between them and the ride home was quiet as well.

When they get back to Harrison's apartment he suggests a movie.

"No, I think I will go to bed I got a flight to catch tomorrow."

"Bahari, your flight doesn't leave until twelve o'clock in the afternoon."

"Well I'm tired goodnight," says Bahari as she goes upstairs into the master suite to get ready for bed.

Harrison takes a seat in the den area, takes his shoes off and turns on the television.

After a few hours and a brief nap on the couch he awakens turns off the television and goes upstairs to get into bed. After he takes off his clothes and puts on his pajama bottoms he climbs into bed with Bahari who is asleep.

He snuggles up next to her and takes in a deep breath of her perfume as he closes his eyes.

Bahari wakes.

"Hey babe I am so sorry to upset you earlier, but I always want to be honest with you, I do love you."

"I know I just never thought that we would see other people."

"Me either, but it could be a good thing. You are on the east coast and I am on the west we are going to be spending a lot of time apart and I just want us both to be happy and not be afraid or feel guilty because we meet other people."

"But I love you."

"And I love you too, but we are not children anymore Bahari."

"I know, but you are the one for me I don't need to see other people to know that."

"I feel that you are the one for me, I just want to be sure beyond a shadow of a doubt. I think that things are different for a man and besides it does not mean that I don't love you."

"What if you meet someone and you like them more than me?"

"Let's cross that road when we get there."

"Okay."

"You're still my princess?"

"Yes."

Harrison reaches over and kisses her deeply, reaches his hand underneath her clothing and fondles her breast.

Bahari is panting heavily as Harrison is kissing her neck, then he takes her breast into his mouth, slides his tongue down her stomach and around her belly button. He reaches for the strings on her pajama pants and Bahari grabs his hand to stop him.

"Harrison I am not sure if I am ready yet."

"We don't have to do anything that you don't want to."

"Would you be mad?"

"Of course not we have waited this long we can wait a little longer, Bahari I love you and that's not going to change."

"You promise?"

"Yes, I have loved you since the sixth grade. We are actually married already remember when Rodney that used to live in the neighborhood married us, his father was a minister and at the time he was the best man for the job, he married us in my tree house?"

"Yes, I do and we stole the rice from your mom's pantry for him and Elise to throw on us."

They both burst into laughter.

"Remember we put foil around our fingers as wedding rings?"

They are both giggling and laughing so hard that Bahari has tears in her eyes as Harrison is grabbing his stomach because he is so tickled.

"We have done some crazy things together."

"Yeah I know."

"And I want plenty more with you Harrison I can't see myself with anyone else. I have known you my whole life."

"I know, let's just see what the future holds. No one is saying we are breaking up; we should be experiencing all kinds of things. We are young and I want no regrets when I do get married I only want to do it once."

"Me, too."

"Do we have an agreement?"

"I guess so. I never looked at it like that before. My mother married my father right out of college and she says she has no idea what it would be like to be with another man, but she did say that there were times that she was curious, but she didn't want to jeopardize her family for it."

"My father says he dated my mother in college, but he did see other women. He had sex with other women just not my mother. My mother was a virgin and she was determined to stay that way until she was married."

"Did your mother know?"

"He says he thinks she did, but she never said anything and he said once they got married he has been faithful to her ever since."

Bahari climbs on top of Harrison and kisses him as her hair falls into his face he gently sweeps it back and kisses her passionately then he turns her so that he is on top.

"I am going to miss you tomorrow."

"I am going to miss you too."

After a few more kisses and laughter from the telling of silly childhood stories they go to sleep in each other's arms.

(The following day at the airport)

They are saying their goodbyes at the airport and Bahari starts to cry when the announcer calls for Bahari's flight to start the boarding process.

"Babe we are going to be fine, I love you."

99

"I love you too. I miss you so much when we are apart."

"I miss you too."

Harrison takes her in his arms and kisses her passionately.

"I feel like I am making a mistake by leaving you alone."

"Babe you have to go back to school call me as soon as you touch down in North Carolina."

"Okay."

"Bye Fathead," says Harrison, a nickname he has called her since they were kids.

Bahari smiles, puts her backpack on her shoulder and blows Harrison a kiss as she walks toward the boarding area, but she never looks back again it was too painful.

Harrison blows a kiss back and he wants so desperately to ask her to stay, but he knows they both have responsibilities and it was time to get back to reality.

Chapter Eight

It has been a couple of weeks since Bahari left and Harrison misses talking to Chutney, but she hasn't called since Bahari came for a visit and he blew her off. He didn't know how she was going to respond therefore he was hesitant to call her.

Harrison decided to reheat his leftover Chinese food and his phone rings.

When he looks at his caller ID he sees Chutney's name and he smiles to himself.

"Hello."

"Hi, stranger."

"Hi, how are you?"

"Can you talk?"

"Sure."

"I thought your girlfriend was still visiting, but then again you wouldn't be answering now would you?"

"I am sorry about that."

"Never mind, what are you up to?"

"I am warming up some leftover Chinese food."

"You?"

"Nothing, I'm bored."

"You want to come over?"

"Sure."

Harrison tells her his address and she tells him she will be there in about an hour.

Chutney hangs up the phone with a smile on her face and rushes to her closet to decide what she was going to wear.

When Chutney arrives at Harrison's condo she is greeted at the door by Harrison in a wife beater and sweatpants.

Chutney knew he had an athletic build, but the wife beater he was wearing showed off his biceps and his chiseled body.

"Hi, did you find me okay?"

"Yes, you gave good directions."

"Come in."

Harrison gives her a hug and closes the door.

"Let's go into the den."

Harrison and Chutney have a seat on the couch.

"I'm sorry can I get you anything?"

"No, I'm fine."

"So what's been up?"

"Nothing much, did you enjoy your visit with your girlfriend?"

"As a matter-of-fact I did."

"Good."

After small talk about weather, upcoming modeling jobs and Harrison's strenuous workout schedule Harrison intervenes.

"Wanna watch a movie?"

"Sure, only if I can pick it out."

"Go ahead."

Chutney walks over to where Harrison's movie collection is and chooses the movie Love Jones.

"Should have known, a chic flick, but that's okay it's a favorite of mine too."

Chutney hands Harrison the movie and he gets up and places it into the DVD player.

"You sure I can't get you anything to drink?"

"What you got?"

Harrison gets up and walks over to the refrigerator and opens it.

"I have some pineapple juice, bottled water, orange juice and a bottlc of wine."

"Wine please."

"Wine it is."

Harrison reaches in the cabinet to get two wine glasses, pops the cork on the wine and pours them each a glass.

Then he carries them over to the couch hands her a glass and has a seat next to her just as the movie starts.

"Thank you."

"Welcome."

They watch the movie each pointing out their favorite scenes, laughing at the amusing scenes and discussing the relationship between men and women and the games that both parties play.

When the movie is over Harrison stands and turns off the television and puts on some jazz music.

"Can I refill your glass?"

"Sure, but this is my last glass."

Harrison just smiles and goes to refill her glass and his own.

They talk more about their families, high school, their hometowns, food and their future plans involving their career choices.

Chutney runs her hands through her hair and pulls it back off of her face.

"You are so pretty to me."

"Thank you."

Harrison sits his glass down, moves a little closer to Chutney and touches her long curly hair.

"You're a hair type of guy aren't you?"

"No, I just think your hair is pretty with all the curls, I like it."

There is a deafening silence as they stare at each other then Chutney moves closer to Harrison and they kiss softly.

They part and without saying a word Harrison grabs her with one hand behind her head, kisses her again more passionately and it lasts a little longer than before.

"Are you sure we should be doing this?"

"Why not, you didn't like it?"

"I did, but you have a girlfriend remember?"

"Yes, we had a talk and we agreed to see other people."

"Really, who brought it up, was it you?"

"Yes, I did. I am feeling some kind of way about you and I don't know why."

"Harrison we just met. I like spending time with you and I don't want to be the reason why you and your girlfriend breakup."

"I assure you, you are not. I just want to explore other options, I don't want to talk about this anymore, you enjoy my company and I enjoy yours so let's just do that, okay."

"Okay, but I don't want to hurt anybody."

"Let me worry about that, okay."

Harrison gives Chutney a quick kiss on the lips.

"I want to show you something."

Chutney reaches for her purse and pulls out an eight by ten vanilla envelope and hands it to Harrison.

Harrison opens it and it is modeling photos of Chutney and he is amazed at how beautiful the pictures are; it appears that she is in the mountains with a beautiful sunrise behind her with no shirt on cupping her breast in her hands with a bikini bottom on looking off into the distance.

In another picture she has on a sheer cover up with the wind in her hair and the cover up is blowing causing it to cling to her body as she looks into the distance with another picture of the same shot, but in that one she has on shades.

"I'm impressed, these are beautiful."

"Thank you."

"When did you take these?"

"A few months ago."

Harrison takes the photos and places them back into the envelope.

"You look totally different in those photos, you are stunningly beautiful. Those were breath taking."

"Thank you, I just need more of them taken. A photographer friend of Tammy's took those."

"He or she did an awesome job."

"He did, but photos like that are really expensive. For a nice photo shoot out here in L.A. you can pay upwards of two-thousand dollars."

"Really."

"Yes, I am saving now to do a shoot with the same guy."

"Wow, it's amazing what a good photographer can do with a good model."

"Who is this guy I need some photos of myself?"

"His name is Randy of La Goddess Dollz."

"I can give you his card he gave me some to give out because he did them at a cut rate price because of Tammy so he just asked that I bring him some business."

Chutney reaches into her purse and hands Harrison Randy's business card.

"I will definitely be calling him I want some pictures of myself on my walls to make it feel more like home for me."

"Make sure you mention me and that I referred you he may take some money off of my pictures when I get all my money together."

"Sure."

Harrison places the business card on the coffee table in front of him.

Chutney places the envelope with the pictures back into her purse and stands.

"Where is your restroom?"

Harrison takes her down the hallway and points to a door leading to the restroom.

Harrison places both wine glasses in the sink and as he is returning to the den area Chutney is coming out of the restroom.

"I better get going its late."

"Okay, well I am glad you came by."

"Me too," says Chutney as she grabs her bag off the couch and walks toward the door.

"You drove?"

"Yes, Tammy let me use her car."

"Okay."

Harrison opens the door to his condo and walks her to her car. Upon their arrival at the car Harrison asks to kiss her again and she obliges.

He makes sure she is safely tucked inside and the doors are locked before she drives away.

As Harrison walks back into his condo he is pleased with the way they interact with each other such as conversation, the things they have in common and the way his body responded to hers as he was sure her body responded to his.

Chapter Nine

It is game night and the Allen and Johnson families are in attendance. Harrison has been spending a lot of time with Chutney but he has ignored her calls because of Bahari and the family visiting. Harrison explained to her as best he could that they were coming and he wasn't going to see her during that time. Chutney said that she understood and her exact words were, "We are just friends right, no strings attached."

The game is off to a good start they are in the lead by eight points and he has racked up three assist.

Harrison is so happy to be in an NBA uniform, his grandmother is in attendance with a proud look on her face. She has been cooking up a storm since she arrived three days ago. Katina has brought him a few pictures of himself playing basketball that were in his bedroom at home to make the condo feel more like home for him.

Bahari has been a little quiet since her arrival with her parents. She says it's because she has a lot on her mind due to some very important tests coming up in school, she brought her books so that she can study.

Mrs. Allen has been shopping everyday and Mr. Allen is complaining about having to pay extra for the extra baggage that they will be traveling back with.

All of them surprised Harrison and had T-shirts made with his number on the back, but Harrison's parents put "Mom" and "Dad" above the number, his grandmother had "Nana" and his grandfather had "Pops" monogrammed on theirs. Harrison was happy to have the support of his family, especially his grandmother, whom was diagnosed with cancer a year ago and it is still in remission.

By the fourth quarter they were up by eighteen points with two minutes left in the game, Harrison now has twenty-two assist and he was proud of those stats and even happier that the team started the season with a win. In the end they won the game 128-114 Clippers win, Harrison scored 14 points.

After the game Harrison meets his family back at the condo where his grandmother has made all his Island favorites the house smelled of jerk and curry seasonings so strong he could smell it as he walked up to his door. The last few days have been fun, but they all leave tomorrow after breakfast.

After a late dinner someone puts a movie in, but Harrison excused himself after the opening credits he was exhausted from the adrenaline of the game. He went into his bedroom and in no time he was asleep, Bahari went in and gave him a kiss on the cheek anyway.

The following morning after his jog, his grandmother made homemade biscuits, scrambled eggs, pancakes, fresh fruit, oatmeal, toast, bacon and sausage.

After breakfast he and Bahari took a short walk because they hardly had any alone time since he had a house full of guest, but they did have fun together. Harrison feels that something was bothering Bahari and that was the real reason for the silence toward him, but she assures him she was okay.

Shortly upon their return the car service was at the condo to take them all back to the airport to take everyone back to their prospective homes: His parents and the Johnson's, Chicago, Bahari, North Carolina and his grandparents, Trinidad. Harrison was a little sad to see them leave, but he was getting used to being on his own for the first time in his life.Besides he would be home in a couple months for the holidays and he was looking forward to that.

Harrison's phone is ringing when he is walking back into the house.

"Hello."

"Hi."

"Congratulations on winning the game."

"Thank you."

"I know your parents were proud."

"Yep."

"Are you okay?"

"Yes, Chutney I am just feeling a little tired and besides my parents and grandparents just left I just want to lie down for awhile."

"Okay."

"I will call you back later."

"Okay, that's cool. Harrison you know you can talk to me about anything."

"Thanks, call you later."

"Bye."

"Bye, pretty lady."

They both release the line.

Tammy comes walking into the living room.

"Hey, what are you getting into today?"

"Nothing I got to go to work shortly."

"Oh, I was hoping we can go to the mall I need a new dress I have been invited to a party this weekend with Terry. Did Harrison invite you?"

"No, he hasn't mentioned anything."

"It's some kind of charity event."

"He told me he has a girlfriend so I guess he doesn't want to be seen with me so that when she comes out to L.A. there will be no eyebrows are raised."

"Do you like him? If so, you better let your feelings be known."

"I like his kindness, thoughtfulness and when he is with you he has a way of making you feel that you are all that matters. I have never met anyone like him."

"Okay so what's the problem?"

"I just feel when we are together that he is holding back."

"Well he probably is, but you have to pull it out of him, haven't I taught you what to do to get your man."

"Well he has a woman."

"Yeah, but you have the power to change that."

"He did tell his girlfriend that he wants to see other people."

"Really, well there is your opening, dear."

"You think so?"

"Yes, when a man says that to you nothing good is coming next. He might as well have said he don't want your behind no more."

"Yes, but even when we kiss I can tell he wants to do more, but he never does and he is so polite about it, he is fine as hell."

"Yes, he is."

"Maybe he is just torn between his feelings for you and this chic."

"I think so and him being the gentlemen he is he doesn't want to hurt either of us. We are just having fun and other than kissing we have not crossed over any boundaries."

"I hope it works out for you because I can tell he likes you, when he came over the other night he was chivalrous; Like sitting after you did, he cleared the table and offered to wash the dishes. When you denied him he helped by drying them, I have never seen that before in my twenty-five years."

They both burst into laughter.

"But that's him, he is just really sweet and I can tell he is a one woman man. I don't think I would have to worry about him like a lot of these other guys especially a ball player. He seems to have been raised to treat a lady with respect."

"You better snap his behind up because he is a rare breed."

"Can you drop me off to work on your way to the mall?"

"Yes ma'am."

"Okay well I am going to start getting ready for work. Thanks for the talk Chica!"

"Anytime."

(Meanwhile)

Harrison is at home he has just awoke from his nap.

His phone rings.

"Hello."

"Hi, Son we just got back. We are so proud of you."

"Thanks Dad. Where is Mom?"

"She says she was going to take a nap."

"Dad I need to talk to you?"

"What's going on?"

"Well Dad I have met a girl since I have been out here and I think I like her."

"Oh, wow. Have you told Bahari?"

"Yes, but not in so many words I ask if we could see other people."

"How did she take that?"

"She at first was mad about it, but I convinced her it was best for the both of us because of the distance between us."

"Me and your mother were wondering how that was going to work out because three years is a long time to wait for someone."

"I know."

"What's her name?"

"Chutney and I don't want to keep her a secret because the more I spend time with her I am really digging her. Dad I do love Bahari, but I feel we are growing apart from each other, or at least I am. I want something different."

"Son, it is your decision. You are a man now and you have to make decisions that are best for you, but the Johnson's nor Bahari going to be happy about this."

"I know, but I want to be happy. Chutney makes me feel a certain way. I can't really explain it. She is a struggling model and I just like her tenacity and the way she has had obstacles in her life, but she continues to fight, I have never met anyone that has her determination."

"Harrison, me and your mom were not born with the golden spoon in our mouths as yourself, but we wanted you to have everything that we did not. The thing is to be sure of your feelings because you don't want to hurt either of them because once you say something son you can't take it back."

"I know Dad and I am worried about Bahari's parents being mad at me."

"Son, don't worry about that, this is your life. Bahari will be mad and so will the Johnson's, but they will be alright."

"You think so."

"Yes."

"Think about your decision. This is really gonna cause trouble, but just like all things it will pass. Pray about it."

"I hope so."

"Have you told your Mom?"

"No, I think she is going to be mad too."

"Probably, you know how fond she is of Bahari."

"I know and that is what is going to make this hard. I love her and the Johnson's, but I want them to respect my decision."

"They will because what can they do about it."

"I guess nothing, I just wish there was an easy way to go about this. I just want Chutney to be comfortable around me and I want to be able to let go of my feelings for her because right now I hold back from her. Dad she is so beautiful and I don't know if she is the one, but I want to be free to do what I want and see whom I want."

"Seems to me your mind is already made up."

"I don't want to feel guilty."

"I understand."

"Thanks for listening to me Dad."

"Anytime, you are my son that's what I'm here for."

"Tell Mom I said I love her."

"I will."

"Love you Dad."

"Love you too, Harrison."

"Bye."

Mr. Allen just hangs up the phone. Harrison just smiles to himself because his Dad never says "Bye."

Chapter Ten

Bahari is in her apartment in Durham, North Carolina that her parents purchased as a gift and when she graduated they would use as income property. She is preparing to go to a Kappa party with her roommate Toni.

"I am glad you are coming with me tonight you have been in a funk since you got back from L.A."

"I know I just feel that Harrison and I are going our separate ways, but you know I am going to move on and try to come to terms with his decision to date other people."

"And you should. I told you most relationships don't survive college especially when the guy is an athlete because of all the female attention they get."

"Well I understand that now, but it wasn't college it was the NBA, evidently the women are just that much more scandalous."

"You think? Not only is he an athlete, but a million dollar athlete. Look Bahari you are a beautiful girl inside and out and you are smart, what man wouldn't want that and besides one day you are going to be a Doctor. Beauty and brains now that's dangerous."

"Thanks I needed that I am going to this party and I am going to have a good time."

"Good and no talk of Harrison tonight."

"Agreed."

The two women shake hands and finish getting dressed.

When they arrive at the party there are party-goers everywhere at the Kappa House and seems as if everyone has a solo cup in their hands.

Bahari and Toni navigate their way through the overly crowded room with the music turned up high blasting Rick Ross' hit "Bag of Money."

Toni sees Greg and goes over to say something to him and leaves Bahari standing alone.

"Hey beautiful what's up," says a voice standing closely behind her in her ear.

Bahari turns around and it is Pierre.

"Hey how are you?"

"I'm good. You are looking good I like that dress and a woman in high heels, now that's sexy."

"Thank you I am sure you tell all the women that."

"No not really, I can tell you were either a cheerleader, a dancer or an athlete because of the way your body is shaped."

"I was a cheerleader."

"I can tell because your calves are strong and those thighs give you away. Can I get you something to drink?"

"Sure I'll take some punch."

"Okay, but you know it's spiked right."

"Yes, I am sure it is."

"I'll be right back."

Bahari and Toni catch each other's eye across the room and Toni mouths, "Are you okay?" and Bahari shakes her head, "yes."

Pierre returns with a solo cup that he hands to her.

"I was surprised to see you here tonight."

"Why?"

"Because I thought you would have been home booed up on the phone with Harrison, your boo."

"Well surprise, I'm not I wanted to get out and have a little fun."

"Well he is not my boyfriend anymore if that's what you are asking."

"When did all this happen?"

"A few weeks ago."

"I knew you guys were going to have trouble once he got drafted because them guys have girls throwing themselves at them and the girls don't care if they are married or have a girlfriend, but you can't blame them they are just living the life."

"Thanks Pierre, you always have a way of making me feel better."

"I didn't mean it like that. I just mean that his circle has expanded and he is in L.A. I am happy for the guy I was just never the athletic type I am more of a gentlemen and a scholar myself, but athletes are like Rock Stars."

"He says he wants to see other people."

"Come on Bahari, did you really think that he was going to stay faithful to you especially after he was drafted?"

"Call me crazy, but yes."

Bahari lowers her head.

"Hey, I didn't mean to make you sad or anything. I know I play around a lot, but you are a nice girl and you are beautiful, rich and smart. I am a nice guy Bahari."

"You are always talking to a lot of girls."

"They are just friends can I help it if girls like me."

"No, but you are not going to add my name to your list of, "Friends.""

"Bahari I already know you are not that type of girl, the type that sleeps around."

"No, I am not."

"I know I am going to have to date you and that's cool, I have always liked you, but I am not ready for a serious relationship I got my studies and so do you."

"True."

"Well since I am in the pharmacy program and you are studying to be a doctor maybe we can meet at the library and study together sometimes."

Bahari raises her eyebrow.

"That's all just study and sometimes we can grab a bite to eat, you gotta eat right?"

"I gotta keep my eye on you and why do you assume that I am rich?"

"Bahari you drive a new expensive car, you always have on designer gear, you have an apartment that I heard your parents spared no expense to decorate and your parents are paying your tuition, unlike myself I am here on financial aid."

"Where did you hear that? Am I supposed to apologize for that, my parents are doctors and I am an only child."

"A little birdie told me and besides I have been inquiring about you since I met you the first week of school, but you had a boyfriend then. Just so you know I was raised by a single parent of three boys and I am the first in my family to go to college, therefore there is a lot that is expected of me, but no pressure."

They both laugh out loud.

"Where is your father?"

"He is around. He wasn't a deadbeat dad or anything him and my mother just didn't work out, he has always been in me and my brother's lives."

"That's good."

After talking a little more about their upbringing, a few jokes, they danced and had a great time until Bahari was ready to leave.

Bahari and Toni were escorted to their car by Greg and Pierre.

"Hey it was nice to get to know you a little better, Bahari I will be taking you up on studying and lunch."

"Okay, but don't try no funny business."

"I promise I won't."

Toni and Greg are saying their goodbyes with a kiss.

"Can I get your number?"

"Sure."

Pierre pulls his cell phone out of his pocket and locks her number in.

"I'll call you tomorrow."

"Cool."

Pierre is walking away from the car as Toni is getting into the car.

"Put your seatbelt on," says Greg.

"Okay," says Toni.

"Call you tomorrow, goodnight ladies, be safe call me and let me know you got back home okay," says Greg.

"I will."

Greg walks away from the car and Bahari drives off.

"You two seem to be getting along great. I have noticed he comes to the apartment more often."

"Yeah, he is really a sweet guy. I really like him he is just really sweet."

"I know you said that already."

"I have a confession," says Toni in a sincere tone.

"What?"

"While you were in L.A. visiting Harrison we had sex."

"Shut up!" exclaims Bahari.

"It was really nice and he wants us to be a couple."

"Okay, so what's the problem?"

"I hate when we go places and people stare at us, it doesn't seem to bother him like it bothers me sometimes I feel like a sale out."

"So people stare. Is he good to you?"

"Yes."

"Well that's all that matters, so what if people stare that's their problem, not yours they are just rude."

"But I don't like it. One night on campus a guy neither one of us knew called me a sale out and he and Greg exchanged words."

"Really, people should be used to interracial couples by now they are everywhere."

"I am wondering what my parents are going to say, Greg says he has always dated women of color so his parents are used to it."

"Really, because usually it is the other way around, it's normally the white parents that are disapproving of their child dating outside of the race."

"My mom and dad are not racist they have just always said that they would prefer if my siblings and I dated within our race, so though I have told them about Greg they assume he is black because I have not told them any different."

"Well if you continue to date him you are going to have to tell them something."

"I know, but enough about me, what about you and Pierre?"

"There is no me and Pierre."

"I saw you give him your number."

"That's so that we can study sometime together."

"You know he has always liked you."

"Yeah, you keep telling me that. Tonight I saw another side of him he has a little depth, he is close to his mom and younger siblings and he is actually funny."

"Yeah, Pierre is cool."

"He is cute too. He has a nice build on him, pretty teeth and a gorgeous smile. I guess I just never really noticed, but that goes to show how much into Harrison I was. I am not ready to get into another relationship as of yet, but I will study with him and maybe go to lunch sometimes."

"Glad to hear it, get on with your life."

They arrive back at the apartment and they both get undressed and are sharing in a carton of Ben and Jerry's

Chunky Monkey ice cream while sitting on Bahari's bed.

"Toni."

"Yeah, wassup."

"I do miss Harrison a lot."

"I know. When was the last time you talked to him?"

"A couple of days ago, we don't talk like we used too."

"That's to be expected."

Bahari is feeling sad her eyes start to fill with tears then she burst into tears.

Toni puts the carton of ice cream down and gives her friend a hug.

"Bahari it is going to be okay and soon you will be back to your old self. Have you told your parents?" "No."

"Why."

"Because they are crazy about him and I am just not ready yet."

"I know it hurts a lot, but you have got to let go, focus on your studies and get yourself together."

"I know, I wanted to call his mother and talk to his mother I just have the feeling that they know because Harrison tells them everything."

"Probably so, but Bahari this is not the end of the world someone else will come along and sweep you off your feet."

Bahari reaches for a piece of tissue beside her bed and blows her nose.

"I bet she is one of those mixed or white girls, her name is Chutney."

"How do you know that?"

"She called a few times when I was visiting him and I questioned him about her. He told me he met her at a party and they went to brunch together."

"So did he say he liked her?"

"No, he says he didn't know because they'd just met. He just said he wanted to see other people."

"That's normally how it starts, they want to see other people then they officially breakup with you when they see that relationship working out for them. She's probably a groupie and you know ball players always want eye candy and you are that, but they want anything that ain't black. She is probably a gold digger too," says Toni in an angry tone.

"He did mention she is a model, so I am sure she is pretty."

"So, I bet she is not prettier than you. I know you have been told this a million times that you look like Jennifer Hudson and what man don't wanna be with Jennifer especially, Jennifer after the weight loss."

The two of them burst into laughter.

"Thanks Toni you are crazy."

"Anytime friend."

After eating the whole carton of ice cream, a few more jokes and a little gossip, Toni retreats to her room and Bahari climbs into her bed and they both go to sleep.

Chapter Eleven

It is December a couple of months since Harrison told Bahari of his decision to see other people and they have not spoken much. Harrison has been seeing as much of Chutney as he can and today she has accompanied him to a photo shoot with her friend,Randya photographer. Harrison will be at an away game in Denver on Christmas Day, then another game on the 27th in Boston, New Year's Eve he is free, but another game in Denver on New Year's Day.

Chutney has taken a seat on a couch in the studio as she watches Harrison take photo after photo.

Harrison is posing in his basketball uniform.

Chutney did step in a few times and give him advice on some poses.

"We are done here I can have the proofs to you in a few weeks, says Randy the photographer.

"Okay, now can you take some of her and me together, maybe just one or two?"

"Harrison I am not prepared to take any photos," says Chutney.

"Oh, stop you look fine," says Harrison as he holds his hand out to her.

"Come on you always look photo ready."

Chutney stands, straighten out her blouse and the scarf around her neck.

"Let me go to the restroom and check my makeup," says Chutney with a smile.

When she returns she goes and stands next to Harrison.

"You are really going to make these pictures look so much better with you in them," whispers Harrison in her ear.

Chutney just smiles and puts his arm around her waist.

After several poses Randy is having a good time taking the photos because they are both photogenic, the camera loves them.

"Can I take a few by myself," asks Chutney.

"That's up to him, but you know those are going to cost you?"

Chutney looks at Harrison and he says, "Go ahead."

Harrison steps to the side and watches while he takes a few of Chutney and she is killing it she even gets her shades and put them on in some of the photos.

When they finish the shoot Harrison puts back on his jeans, shirt and jacket. He joins Randy and Chutney in a sitting area so that they may discuss his deposit.

"I had fun with you guys today. Harrison let me give you some cards to give out to some of the players on the team I am trying to build my clientele. Send me some clients and I'll give your girl here a discount," says Randy.

"Cool, thanks," says Harrison as he looks at Chutney.

Randy reaches for his camera on the couch and shows Harrison some of the shots he took of him and some that included Chutney.

"I like them, my mom is going to love them," says Harrison.

"I am sure she will, maybe you can use some of them as promo shots as well make them into 4x6 sign them and give them away to fans," suggested Chutney with a smile.

"I like that you suggested the baby oil and sprit-zing me with water or should I say when you had her do it," says Harrison with a smile as he pats Chutney on the thigh," says Harrison with a smile.

"Well I wasn't gonna do it. When you come to proof them the ones you decide to do that with can I please put my logo in a corner of the photo," asks Randy.

"Sure, that's a good idea," says Harrison.

"Today your deposit is $500.00," says Randy.

"Do you take credit cards?" asks Harrison as he reaches in his pocket for his wallet.

"Yes," says Randy and he reaches on the table to get his square card reader and attaches it to his phone.

Harrison hands him his card and Randy swipes it and hands his phone to him for him to sign his name.

"How much would it be for me to get some head shots and more photos for her?" asks Harrison.

"That depends on the shoot. What kind of shoot do you want?" asks Randy as he looks at Chutney and Chutney is looking at Harrison.

"Well you said you needed some photos," says Harrison.

"I do," says Chutney.

"He just asked you a question," says Harrison as he looks at her with a smile.

"Thank you," says Chutney then she turns to Randy.

"I want location shots maybe the beach or a park, I need some high fashion shots?" says Chutney squealing with excitement.

"Okay I got some ideas. I will need a deposit to put her on the books," says Randy.

"How much?" asks Harrison

"Another $500.00," informs Randy.

Harrison passes his credit card back to him.

After Randy swipes Harrison's Visa card again and makes an appointment for Chutney's photo shoot, they leave the studio.

"Thank you so much, you are so kind I really appreciate it."

"You are welcome."

Chutney grabs Harrison's hand as they walk to the car and she stops and kisses him on the lips.

"Thank you, I really mean that."

"You are welcome, I like doing things for you so that I can see that gorgeous smile and your eyes just light up when you are happy."

"Why are you so nice to me?"

"Why are you so nice to me?"

They stand and stare at each other for awhile in silence.

"Can I cook you dinner tonight?"

"Yes, you can and I hope you mean at my house."

"I do."

"Do you have to be at work today?"

"No, I am off today."

"Great, because day after tomorrow I have an away game, we have to stay at the hotel tomorrow and I'd like to spend some time with you."

"Okay."

Chutney smiles at him and they get in his car and drive away.

Chutney has the kitchen smelling good she is preparing grilled rib eye steaks, homemade whipped herbed potatoes topped with cheese and grilledasparagus.

Harrison comes into the kitchen as she is preparing the plates.

"Can I help?"

"Yes, you can set the table."

Harrison sets the table and opens a bottle of wine as Chutney is putting the plates on the table.

They both take a seat and Harrison grabs her hand to say grace.

"Everything looks and smells so good."

"Thank you."

Harrison cuts a piece of his steak and it is medium well, just the way he likes it and puts it into his mouth.

"Mmmmm this is so tender and seasoned well too, she cooks and she's beautiful, check."

137

"I told you I always had to watch my younger siblings because my mother worked all the time therefore I did most of the cooking and the cleaning."

"She taught you well."

"Some of it, I got tired of eating the same thing all the time so I was always online looking for recipes and watching cooking shows, I like cooking. I do all of the cooking with Tammy she has no Idea how to boil a hotdog."

They both laugh.

After dinner Harrison cleared the table and put the dishes in the dishwasher.

The two of them have a seat on the couch.

"You were such a natural today at the shoot."

"Well I'm the model remember."

"I hope that when you send those photos out to agencies that you get a call because as beautiful as you are you should be working."

"I am keeping my fingers crossed."

"I will make sure I say a prayer for you."

"That was really sweet to say."

"No problem, as I was watching you today I was just mesmerized by how comfortable you are in front of a camera and that alone is a talent. I never liked taking pictures it makes me uncomfortable."

"I have always liked the camera even as a kid my Papa, grandfather, used to take pictures of me it was a hobby of his and he said between me and my sister I had the gift and he always said being beautiful doesn't mean you will take a good picture it's in the face, the body and the mind."

"You and your grandfather are really close, huh. You talk about him a lot."

"Yes, and I was crushed when he died in my senior year of cancer, I promised him I was going to become a model, a household name."

Chutney lowers her head.

"It has been hard for me being out here with no family and no support, don't get me wrong Tammy has been like a sister to me and I am grateful to her, but there are times when I just want to go back home, get a job get married and settle for a simple life."

Harrison takes his hand and lifts her head up.

"Would that make you happy?"

"Of course not, I want something better for myself and for my kids. I want better than what my mother did for me, though she did what she could. I just want to offer my sisters, brother and nephew a better life. I want my sister to get into rehab and get her life on track and be a mother to her son."

"Make that what drives you. I am sure a lot of models have your same story. I will help you as much as I can."

"Thank you, when I ask you earlier why are you so nice to me, you never answered and I'd like to have an answer."

"Because you deserve it, that's why."

Harrison kisses her softly as he moves closer to her on the love seat.

Chutney climbs on top, straddles him and they kiss passionately.

After a while Harrison picks her up and carries her into his bedroom and places her gently on the bed as they are kissing Harrison's cell phone is ringing.

"Do you want to get that?"

"No, whoever it is they can wait."

They both smile at each other.

Harrison gets on top of her moves his hand up under her shirt and fondles her breast, lifts up her shirt, takes her breast out of her bra and takes her breast into his mouth.

Chutney lets out a moan.

Harrison then slowly unbuttons her blouse as he is looking her directly in the eyes.

"We don't have to do this if you don't want to?"

"I want to."

"Are you sure?"

"Yes, I feel like I am finally with a nice man. Where I come from they are few and far in between, they just want to have sex."

"I want more from you than that, I like spending time with you."

"I like spending time with you too."

They both get undress and Chutney climbs on top of him. As she is kissing him on his chest she can feel his heart racing.

"Are you okay?"

"Yes, I'm a little nervous that's all."

"We don't have too, I know you and your girlfriend are still friends and if you are not ready we can wait."

"Chutney I have something to tell you."

"What   is   it?"
Chutney sits on top of him straddling him.

"I'm a virgin."

"You are kidding right?"

"No, I am not. I am just so attracted to you and I want to do it, but I am nervous."

"SHHHH."

Chutney slides down on top of him and kisses Harrison on the lips, his neck, then his chest.

Harrison lets out a loud moan of ecstasy they make love passionately.

"How was I?"

"You were nice and gentle they way a woman likes it. I am not surprised because you are soft spoken, kind and sweet. Harrison it was beautiful."

"Thank you, you are too."

They kiss, Harrison pulls her closer to him and they spoon as he holds her in his arms.

After a little conversation they have sex again, afterwards they go into the kitchen for some fruit and bottled water, they climb back into bed.

When Chutney falls asleep Harrison stares at her as he plays with her hair.

"I am going to take care of you," says Harrison softly as he kisses her gently on the cheek.

(The Morning)

Chutney awakes and for a moment she forgets where she is then she puts a smile on her face on the pillow next to her there is a note that reads:

Chutney,

I really enjoyed you last night take your time you can leave whenever you want. Just turn on the espresso machine it makes coffee automatically I've already set it up for you. Whenever you are ready to leave I have left instructions for the doorman to call you a car and the chauffeur will take you wherever you want to go.

You look so pretty sleeping I didn't want to wake you, I won't be back I have to check into the hotel. I will see you when I get back. I'll call you tonight.

Take Care,

Harrison

Chapter Twelve

Bahari is at her apartment and pondering the thought of calling Harrison, but is not sure if she should or not, they have not spoken in two weeks. The anticipation is killing her, she walks over and picks up her cell phone and dials his number.

"Hello."

"Hi, Harrison it's Bahari, did I disturb you?"

"No, how are you, I was going to call and check on you, but I have just been so busy."

"How are you, I miss you."

"I miss you too. I just have a lot going on with all the games and practices I am just really busy."

"Are you still seeing your friend?"

"Bahari, do we have to talk about this?"

"I just wanted to know and from what you are saying, you are."

"Yes, I am if you must know."

"Harrison, am I suppose to just sit around and wait for you, I feel I can't move on because this is still unresolved. What are we going to do?"

"I don't know I am confused because I know I still have feelings for you."

"Do you have feelings for her?"

"Bahari, I would rather wait to have this conversation when we are face-to-face, can this wait?"

"No, I have been on hold long enough and I am ready to go on with my life. Are you going to be my man and we move forward with our plans or are we moving in different directions?"

"I can't answer that right now."

"Well I will make the decision for you, you are selfish and I am not going to put up with it anymore. I have given you enough time to make up your mind."

"Bahari don't do this."

"Do what? Allow you to take control of my life, well no more. Harrison as much as this hurts me to say, I am done. Thanks for nothing."

"Bahari I never meant to hurt you, you mean a lot to me."

"Well you have, but I can't be mad with you I have allowed it. I should have known when you asked me about seeing other people I should have put my foot down then, but its okay it was a lesson learned."

"I wish you did not feel that way. I was trying to be honest with you."

"Sure you were and there is no telling what else you have been doing with her and like a fool I am sitting here waiting on you to make up your mind. Have you kissed her?"

"Bahari."

"Bahari what, just answer the question."

Harrison is silent.

"Harrison, are you there?"

"Yes, I am. To answer your question, yes I have and I am sorry."

"Harrison I never would have thought that we would end up like this. You are just like all the rest. When were you going to tell me? For all I know you have had sex with her too."

"I was going to call you, I'm sorry."

"You are sorry, have you had sex with her?"

"Bahari I have to go I am not going to get into this with you."

"Harrison, you did didn't you?"

Harrison is silent. Bahari hears him clearing his throat.

"I can't believe you. I trusted you and this is how you betray me? I can't believe how wrong I was about you."

"You can trust me I have always been there for you, I just think we are going in different directions and I met someone that I am interested in, it just happened and I'm sorry. It does not mean that I don't love you because I do just in a different way."

"I love you too, but I have to get on with my life. It's clear you have moved forward with yours."

"You are my best friend we have been through so much together."

"Evidently not enough because the first time that we are separated you quickly go and jump into bed with someone else."

"It did not happen like that please, I want to be friends."

"I can't do that right now and that is something you should have thought about when you were kissing and having sex with her."

Bahari starts to cry.

"Bahari, please don't cry."

"I can't believe you gave your virginity to someone that looks at you as a piece of meat, she is probably a groupie. Harrison I love you."

"I love you too."

Bahari is crying, "I can't do this, I wish you well."

"Can we be friends?"

"Not right now, you have hurt me really bad Harrison."

"Bahari."

Harrison hears her crying harder and then the phone goes dead. Harrison tries calling her back several times, but she does not answer.

Harrison decides to send her a text that reads:

I am sorry and I hope that you can find it in your heart to one day forgive me. My intentions were never to hurt you. If you want to talk I am here for you. You are a beautiful, smart and a sweet person some lucky man will benefit from my mistake one day.

After about 30 minutes Bahari responds with a text that reads:

Please do not contact me anymore.......

Harrison is surprised at her text, but he decides to obey her request. Just thinking about the situation makes him sad. He sits back in his chair and closes his eyes and tears start to form.

After a few moments Harrison phone rings again.

"Hello," says Harrison as he clears his throat.

"Hi, how are you?"

"Hi, Chutney I'm good."

"What's wrong?"

"Nothing I just got off the phone with Bahari and she is not taking the breakup well. I feel bad."

"I am sorry I just hope that I had nothing to do with that."

"You didn't."

"Is there anything I can do?"

"No, I'll be okay we have been friends since we were kids and I will miss her."

"Have you told your parents yet?"

"I talked to my dad about it."

"What did he say?"

"Not much, just that it is my life and make decisions that feel right for me."

"He is right you know. I was in a relationship with a guy when I came to L.A. but I broke it off because we are on different sides of the world and I felt I needed to be free to do what I wanted and besides neither of us had the means to keep a long distance relationship going."

"Do you still have feelings for him?"

"No. Not other than a friend he still calls me every so often. He was angry with me in the beginning, but we are friends now and he is supportive of me and my career."

"I hope one day that Bahari and I can get to that understanding, because she really is a nice person. I feel like I am experiencing a death."

"I know how you feel because I felt the same way. We had been friends since we were in middle school, but he is involved now with a girl that used to be my best friend."

"How do you feel about that?"

"It hurt at first, but life is strange and I am no longer mad with either of them, because I want a modeling career more than anything and I am not going to let anything stand in my way."

"I like that you are so focused."

"You are too when it comes to playing basketball."

"Yes."

"I can't wait to see you when you back."

"Me too, I am glad that now everything is out in the opening.

Chapter Thirteen

It is Christmas Day in Denver, Colorado and Harrison is celebrating with his family. His mom and dad along with his grandparents have flown in to watch the game and spend the holiday with Harrison. The Clippers won the game at the buzzer 148-147.

Harrison has rented a cabin for the holiday festivities. Tina, Harrison's mom has cooked Pastelles a corn meal patty stuffed with beef, capers, olives and raisins, fried garlic pork, baked ham, stew chicken, rice and peas, ponche creame; a rum and raw egg milk drink, black cake and coconut sweet bread.

After they bless the food everyone immediately start to pass bowls of food around and once everyone has their plates filled there is much conversation and laughter.

"Where is Bahari? I thought that she and her parents would be here," asks Gwenn.

"They went to Antigua, they are meeting some family and friends there," says Mrs. Allen.

"I was looking forward to seeing Bahari, she is such a sweet chile," says Gwenn.

"Grandma me and Bahari are no longer together," says Harrison as he puts some chicken in his mouth with a funny look on his face.

"What, when dis happen?" asked Gwenn in a concerned voice.

The chatter at the dinner table has seized and everyone is waiting for Harrison's answer.

Harrison clears his throat.

"Well I am on the west coast and she is on the east coast and I feel it is for the best. I don't want her sitting around waiting on me. We are young and we should be dating and having fun," says Harrison trying to sound convincing because he knows he is the reason for the breakup.

"Harrison what is going on?" asks Tina in a demanding voice.

"Mom I want to explore other options that's all," responds Harrison.

"There is more going on here than what you are saying," says Gwenn as she puts a piece of ham in her mouth and looking at Harrison suspiciously.

"Momma, Tina it's the boy's decision," says Mr. Allen in a stern voice.

"Allen is right. Leave the boy be, he is man now and can make his own de-ci-sion," says Grandpa Deveaux in his thick island accent. Grandpa Deveaux is a man of few words.

"I liked her, how is she? I am sure she is heartbroken," says Tina.

"Give her time she will be okay it's been awhile. I am sure she is going to be okay," says Mr. Allen.

"What are you saying, you knew about this?" asks Tina.

Mr. Allen clears his throat and looks over at Harrison.

"Harrison called me when we got back from L.A. and told me about it," says Mr. Allen.

"Why didn't you tell me?" asks Tina.

"Mom I knew you would react this way," says Harrison.

"Oh my goodness I guess that's why when I saw Bahari's mom at the store and when I called her the other day to wish them a happy holiday and safe trip she was short with me. I thought she was just caught up in the hustle and bustle of the holidays. She probably assumes that I knew about this," says Tina.

"I guess she has told her parents by now, but I was hoping it would not affect your relationship with them," says Harrison.

"I called her dad the other day for a game of golf and he was short with me, but I let it go they will come around. I am not surprised at how they have reacted to the news

153

of the breakup but when they do decide to speak with us about it I plan to tell them it's Harrison's decision, not ours and that I stand behind his decision," says Mr. Allen.

"Is there someone else?" asked Gwenn as she stared Harrison square in the eyes.

Harrison is quiet, puts his fork down and sits back in his chair.

"Grandma if you must know, yes," says Harrison sounding irritated.

"I knew it. This is what I was afraid of," says Gwenn.

"Woman leave the boy be. All dem girls coming at him all de time, what is he pose to do?" asked Grandpa Deveaux.

"Besides who Harrison chooses as a girlfriend is his choice and not ours," Mr. Allen.

"All I am saying is that Bahari was family and it is going to take a lot to fill her shoes. She is beautiful, smart and just a sweet girl," says Mrs. Allen.

"I liked that with her we knew what we were getting she was not after his money, she really loved him. I want him to meet someone that has his best interest at heart and truly loves him for him is all," says Grandma Gwenn.

"Okay enough of talk about that, Harrison is grown now and we all want to protect him, but he has to make decisions that are best for him and we have to support that no matter what," says Mr. Allen.

"You're right and baby we stand behind you no matter what. I am just hoping that her parents feel the same way," says Mrs. Allen.

After eating, opening gifts, watching basketball, eating again and playing cards they all went to bed except for Harrison because he and Chutney were on the phone until 4 a.m.

Chapter Fourteen

When Harrison got back to L.A. after a string of wins while on the road the first person he called to say he was home was Chutney. She squealed with excitement. She had been anxiously awaiting his return especially when he told her he had a surprise for her.

Harrison is at his condominium when he hears the door bell ring. He has sent a car for Chutney and has been anxiously awaiting her arrival.

Harrison opens the door of his condo and says, "Hey you."

"Hi, how are you?"

"I am better now."

They hug.

She steps into the doorway and Harrison closes the door behind her.

Harrison takes her purse and leads her by the hand to the dining room table and pulls her chair out for her.

"Something smells good."

"I ordered some ribs, potato salad, garlic bread, baked beans and picked up a cheesecake from the bakery, so I hope you are as hungry as I am."

"Yummy, I am. I didn't eat anything today except for breakfast."

Harrison goes into the kitchen to bring the food to the table then he takes a seat across from her.

Harrison blesses the food and they both dig in.

"I like the way you have your hair pulled up its pretty like that."

"Thanks, I am glad you like it."

"I do. Did you do it yourself?"

"No, Tammy did and she helped me pick out my dress."

"Tell her I said she did a good job."

"I will."

"I missed you."

"Really, what did you get me?"

"Can we eat first?"

"Sure, but you know you didn't have to buy me anything."

"I know that, but I wanted to."

"I thought about you a lot while you were gone."

"Yeah, what did you think?"

"I was thinking how kind and nice you are to me and I want this to go slow because we are both trying to get somewhere in our careers."

"I have a question for you."

"Okay."

"How was I when we had sex I have been curious about that because it was my first time?"

"Believe me you are fine in that department you made love to me as if you were in love with me. A lot of men are not as attentive and tender and though it was your first time you took your time."

"So were you satisfied with me? You are all that I could think about while I was gone. I really like you." Chutney smiles at him. Harrison moves in for a kiss.

Chutney pushes her chair back, removes her napkin from her lap and places on the table and walks over to him. Harrison pushes his seat back from the table and she straddles him.

Harrison kisses her passionately and slowly puts his hand under her dress and grabs her buttocks and squeezes them. Chutney lets out a sigh of relief.

Harrison stands and carries her into his bedroom and he slowly undresses her and makes love to her.

"Wait right here."

Chutney smiles and sits up in bed.

When Harrison returns he has a small brown box with a pink bow tied around it.

Harrison sits on the side of the bed and hands it to her.

"What is it?"

"Open it and see, and No it is not a ring."

They both burst into laughter.

Chutney slowly takes the bow off as she stares Harrison in the eyes. When she opens the box it is a pair of diamond earrings.

"Harrison, Oh my God they are so beautiful."

"Just like you."

"Awwwwe thanks I love them." Chutney gives Harrison a big hug and passionate kiss.

"Are you going to put them on?"

"Sure."

She takes off the cubic zirconium earrings she has on and puts on the real deal then she gets out of bed and goes into the bathroom to look into the mirror with Harrison following closely behind her.

She is in awe when she sees herself in the mirror Harrison is standing behind her with his arms wrapped around her.

Chutney stares in the mirror at her and Harrison as her eyes begin to fill with tears.

"Hey what is the matter, you should be happy," says Harrison as he turns her around to wipe her eyes.

"I am. It's just that no one has ever been as nice to me as you have."

"Well get used to it because I plan on spoiling you."

Chutney puts her arms around him and gives him a passionate kiss then she drops to her knees to show him her appreciation.

Harrison has seen this type of sexual act done in movies, but has never experienced it and he is blown away by how good it feels.

After they shower together they lie in bed holding each other until they both fall asleep.

(Morning)

Harrison awakes to Chutney making him pancakes, bacon and sausage with a large glass of orange juice.

"Breakfast in bed, I must have done something right because my mom and grandma are the only two women that have ever served me in bed."

"Well get used to it because if you keep doing things right I may even throw in some lunches and dinners too."

"Come here."

Chutney reaches down to him and he kisses her softly.

"Good morning."

"Good morning, what are your plans for today because I have to be at work at 2:00?"

"Really I thought that we could stay in watch movies, play some games and catch lunch and dinner later."

"I have to go to work sorry, but maybe when I get off I can come back because I am off tomorrow and we can spend the day together."

"Tomorrow I have a team meeting and practice so I won't be here until later on in the evening. Hey I wanted to talk to you about maybe starting up a charity. Many athletes have them and my Agent is on me about getting more involved with the community."

"I think that is a great idea, what do you feel passionate about?"

"I have always wanted to work with kids in the inner city to provide them with scholarships and teach them the fundamentals of basketball along with an annual summer camps. I want to encompass more black male leadership, teach young black men in the inner city how to dress and tie a tie, how to show good sportsmanship on and off the court, tutoring etc."

"Okay, that sounds good."

"I think I will, but I need a building first."

"I am sure your agent can help you with that."

"He can, but I was thinking about you."

"Me, I don't know anything about starting a charity."

"I don't either, but I am really busy. You could quit your job because I know you hate waitressing and come and work for me. I will hire you the best advisors and even have my mom to assist you as well.

My mom has been talking about doing something to keep her busy. I can get her to assist with the counseling side of things."

"Are you serious? I don't come cheap you know."

They both laugh.

"I am sure you don't, but just think about it. I don't have to have an answer right now."

"I will do that."

"One more thing, do you have to go to work today, can you please take the day off?"

Chutney looks at him and smiles because she was thinking it, but did not want to say it.

"I will call in and see what my manager says we are usually not too busy on Sundays."

Chutney goes downstairs and gets her cell phone out of her purse and calls her job.

She returns upstairs and jumps on the bed.

"Now what did you say you wanted to do today."

Harrison places the tray of food on the floor throws her back on the bed and tickles her.

They spend the rest of the day watching movies, playing games, ordering take-out and enjoying each other's company.

Chapter Fifteen

(One year later)

Harrison House Inc., a non-profit program for inner city kids is a day away from its Grand Opening. Chutney is spewing instructions and how she wants everything to be for Grand Opening day.

Chutney has invited the media, city officials, other athletes, celebrities and some local talent out for food, fun and entertainment. Harrison being the kid he is also hired clowns, face painters and a cotton candy booth for the kids as well as a bouncy house.

Chutney and Harrison's mom Katina hit it off well when they met and were able to work together to make the event special for Harrison and especially the children in the inner city neighborhoods. Harrison has secured buses for those parents and children that don't have vehicles.

Harrison is very pleased to see the work that Chutney and his mom have pulled together and he is most pleased by the fact that his mother has made an effort to get to know her, but the real test comes when his grandmother and grandfather arrive.

Katina did not hesitate when Harrison asked her to L.A. to help with the organizing, designing and setting up the structure as to the day to day business of the charity.

Chutney and Katina even went shopping for outfits for the occasion.

"Thanks baby everything looks so nice," says Harrison as he looks around the room in admiration.

"Well most of this was your mother's idea she really has an eye for design and fund raising," says Chutney as she looks around the room to admire her and Mrs. Katina's work.

"My dad says the same thing. My Mom does a blood drive every year for the hospital he works for and a annual fund raiser, she practically, through the funds of other's built the children's heart wing of the hospital," says Harrison with a smile.

"I like her, I can learn a lot from her," says Chutney.

"Yeah, that's my Mom," says Harrison with a smile as he reaches down to give Chutney a kiss.

"Mom, thanks so much for helping me out, the place looks so nice. I cannot wait until tomorrow," says Harrison.

"I gotta go and get your dad from the airport. I'll see you back at the house. Thanks Chutney for helping me pick out my dress, I love it," says Mrs. Katina.

"No problem Mrs. Katina. Your husband is going to love it too," says Chutney with a smile.

"Mom I sent a car to get Grandma and Grandpa so that we don't have to go back to the airport. Chutney and I are going to dinner tonight so don't worry about cooking anything for me," says Harrison.

"Okay, see you later, Harrison and see you tomorrow Chutney," says Mrs. Allen as she gives them both a hug.

"Are you ready for tomorrow?"

"Yes, I went today and picked up my suit and shoes and I think I know my presentation down to a tee."

"You will be fine," says Chutney as she gives him a hug around his waist.

Since Chutney took the job to help establish Harrison House she has been able to send more money home to help her mother and she was able to quit her waitressing job that she hated anyway.

"We need to go so that we can get out of here and get dressed for dinner."

"Okay I just have a few more things I need to tell the kitchen staff and lock up the offices in the rear and I will be ready."

"Okay I am going to take another look around the playground."

"Meet you in the front in twenty minutes?"

"Yes."

Harrison gives her a kiss then they head in different directions.

(The next afternoon)

Harrison is beaming with pride when he asks the mayor of the city to help in cutting the ribbon to Harrison House.
Once the ribbon is cut all the guest some 200 or more are all ushered in from the red carpet, the media is capturing the event with interviews to be shown on tonight's news, there is radio and local newspaper coverage as well.

They were all taken on a tour of the building as Harrison explains what the purpose of each of the rooms will be including the play areas outside. Then dinner was served.

All the guest were treated to grilled shrimp, ribs, chicken, rice and peas, salad, Mac-n-cheese, greens, green beans and for dessert there was pound cake, cupcakes, cookies, cake pops, sweet potato pie, apple pie and pecan pie.

The adults as well as the kids seemed to be having a good time.

Harrison after he has eaten goes to the podium to make an announcement and asks Chutney to come with him. They walk together holding hands.

"Can get your attention please," asks Harrison of all his guests as he clangs on a glass half filled with water.

"I would like to thank the media, friends, teammates, guest and especially the children for helping me make Harrison house a reality for me and the community. I want to thank this lovely lady standing next to me, Chutney as well as my mother, Katina Allen for designing and working tirelessly on the building, you guys did a wonderful job. Mom, Dad, Grandma and Grandpa please stand."

They all stand and the guest clapped.

"Who is Chutney, is that your girlfriend?" asked a member of the press.

Harrison looks at Chutney and smiles.

"I'm not sure maybe that is something you should ask her, Chutney," says Harrison as he pulls her to the mic.

"I'm not sure," says Chutney with a smile as she looks back at Harrison.

Harrison steps up to the mic.

"Maybe she doesn't know because I have never formally asked her, Chutney will you be my girlfriend?"

The whole room is filled with smiles and waiting for her answer, especially his parents and grandparents. Grandma Gwenn is keeping an eye on her because from the outside she seems to be a nice girl but she has yet to get to know her. Grandpa Deveaux was captured by her beauty and immediately liked her. The kids in the room giggled and some of them loudly objected with "ewwww." Some of the women in the room from the looks on their faces were envious.

"I don't know what to say?"

The crowd in the room said in unison, "Say Yes."

"I guess it's a yes, then."

Harrison gives her a kiss and the room explodes into laughter and cheers.

Tammy is beaming with joy. She is happy for Chutney and she adores Harrison for the way he treats her, but most of all she is hoping they move in together and she can have her townhome back to herself.

"These lovely ladies you see standing to my left and my right are holding satchels. They are going to be passing them around to take donations."

The ladies then start to pass the satchels around from table to table as the guest including Harrison's parents start to fill them full of checks.

"We are also taking donations on our website at harrisonhouse.org," informs Chutney as she smiles at the crowd and winks at Harrison.

"Thank you all for coming out," says Harrison as the ladies make their way back to the podium. Two muscular men walk with the ladies to the back office.

Harrison and Chutney go back to their table.

After Harrison played with the kids and made sure they all got a gift bag before getting back on the buses, saying goodbye to press and all the other guests and thanking them again for coming out he was ready to call it a night.

"I am so proud of you," says Chutney to Harrison.

"Thank you, you helped me make it possible."

Harrison's parents and Grandparents walk up.

"We are so proud of you Son," says Mr. Allen.

"Thanks Dad."

They all have a group hug.

"Chutney thanks for helping our baby do all of this," says Grandma Gwenn with a smile as she looks around the room as the cleaning crew is working to clean up the room.

"Thank you, but it was Mrs. Katina that did most of the work," says Chutney.

Chapter Sixteen

Harrison and Chutney arrive in Tennessee for a family visit for her birthday. They check into a hotel then they head to her mother's house.

It is a small house in the Garden View area of town and when Harrison arrives he sees why Chutney was in a rush to leave. There were burglar bars on the windows and doors and there seemed to be a liquor store on every corner.

When they arrived in their rental car the residents of the area were staring at them because they knew the car did not belong in their neighborhood.

Chutney asks Harrison to wear a ball cap and some shades so that he can conceal his identity being that he is a well known player for the Clippers and he could be a target to get them robbed.

"Hi Mom," says Chutney with a big smile.

"Hey I am so happy to see you," says Daniela, Chutneys mom as she opens the wrought iron door and welcomes them in.

Daniela and Chutney hug.

Daniela is a short thin woman, whom appears to be in her early forties, long brown hair and a tan complexion.

You can tell when she was young she was a beauty it is clear where chutney gets her looks from.

"Mommy this is Harrison," says Chutney.

"Hello I have heard a lot about you," says Daniela, Chutneys mom.

"Hello Ma'am, it is nice to meet you," says Harrison with a smile as he leans forward to give her a hug.

"Call me Daniela, everyone else does," says Daniela.

Her little brother Reshawn was running to her then stopped in his tracks when he saw Harrison and stared at him.

"Chutney who is this?" asked Reshawn.

"This is my friend Harrison, say hello."

"Hi Harrison," says Reshawn in a low tone.

"Hey, little man how are you?" asked Harrison as he puts his hand up to give him a high five.

"I am good," says Reshawn and gives Harrison a high five.

Chutney reaches down and gives Reshawn a kiss.

"I missed you, you been taking care of mommy?" asked Chutney.

"Yes," says Reshawn.

"Where is Savaughn?" asked Chutney.

"He is taking a nap you know he is evil when he is sleepy," says Daniela.

"Where is Michelle?" asks Chutney.

"She is at a neighbor's house she said to call her when you arrived, come in and have a seat."

Harrison, Chutney and Reshawn go into the living room area.

There are crucifixes on the wall and pictures of Mary and baby Jesus, a blue couch and loveseat, lots of pictures of each of the kids' accomplishments and many baby pictures, a 42 inch television sitting on an old table.

The front door opens and in walks a very excited Michelle.

"Where is Chutney," says Michelle as she storms into the living room.

Chutney stands up and gives her sister a hug.

"Look at you, you are growing up so fast and your hair is getting so long," says Chutney.

"I love the pictures you sent me, I'm gonna be a model too," says Michelle with a big smile. Michelle has long, thick, curly hair; she is 5 foot 6 inches, thin with brown eyes.

"Michelle I want you to meet Harrison, my boyfriend," says Chutney.

"Hi," says Michelle as she reaches out her hand.

"Hello Michelle, nice to meet you," says Harrison as he stands to give her a handshake.

Savaughn walks into the living room.

"Michelle," says Savaughn with his arms out.

"Hey Savaughn," says Chutney with a smile and she walks over and picks him up.

Chutney kisses him and he lays his head on her shoulder.

"I am so glad that you are home, how long are you going to be here?" asks Michelle.

"Just three days I wanted to see you guys for my birthday," says Chutney as she sits down with Savaughn on her lap. When Harrison says hello to Savaughn he turns his head away from him.

"He is not very friendly with strangers," says Chutney.

"You guys come and eat," yells Daniela.

"You guys go and wash your hands, take Savaughn with you," says Chutney as she stands up and puts Savaughn down.

The kids go to the restroom to wash up for dinner.

"Your family is nice and whatever your mother is cooking it smells good," says Harrison.

"I am glad you came with me, tomorrow we will go sightseeing. Come on let's go to the kitchen and see what's cooking," says Chutney as she grabs his hand as they go to the kitchen.

"Mom you need any help," says Chutney as they stand in the doorway of the kitchen.

"I can help too I can set the table," says Harrison.

The kids come into the kitchen.

"Michelle you set the table and Chutney, help me bring all the dishes to the table," says Daniela.

"Harrison let me show you the bathroom so you can wash up," says Chutney.

When Chutney returns to the kitchen her mother is stirring a pot of black bean soup.

"Hand me a bowl so that I can put this soup in then take it to the table," says Daniela.

"What do you think of him Mom," says Chutney as she hands her mother a bowl and she fills it with soup.

"He seems to be a nice guy, you look happy," says Daniela.

"Thanks Mom," says Chutney as she takes the bowl and brings it to the table.

Harrison comes to the table and Chutney instructs him where to sit.

Chutney brings out the rest of the meal; Arroz con pollo, a popular chicken and rice dish seasoned with adobo and various herbs and spices, greens flavored with smoked neck bones and ham, corn bread and tostones, crispy fried plantains slices.

Chutney is very pleased with the meal; her mother has made all of her favorites. Chutney sits down at the table next to Harrison with a smile on her face.

Daniela comes from the kitchen carrying non-alcoholic sangria, with pineapple, orange, strawberry and lemon slices floating on top.

"Everything looks so good," says Harrison.

"Thank you," says Daniela as she takes her seat at the table.

Daniela says a prayer over the food and they all pass the dishes filled with food and begin enjoying their meal.

"So Harrison, how many brothers and sisters do you have," asks Daniela.

"I am an only child ma'am," responds Harrison.

"Who did you play with?" asks Reshawn quizzically.

"I had friends," said Harrison with a smile.

"What do your parents do for a living?" asks Daniela.

"They are both Doctors," says Harrison.

"How did you grow so tall, you are a giant?" asks Reshawn.

"I don't know I just kept growing," responds Harrison with a smile.

"I saw you on television playing basketball. I am going to play basketball," says Reshawn.

"Really maybe tomorrow you can show me what you got," says Harrison.

Reshawn looks at him and smiles.

"I can't believe you are twenty years old today," says Daniela as she looks at Chutney with a smile.

"Mom don't start, we have company," says Chutney.

"Yeah, Mom, you cry for everybody's birthday," says Michelle.

"Harrison where are you from?" asks Daniela.

"Chicago," says Harrison.

"Oh, the windy city," says Daniela.

"I call it the land of Oprah, I love her, have you ever met her?" asks Michelle.

"No I haven't, but I would like to," says Harrison.

"She is super rich and she is smart, she tells everybody what to do," says Michelle.

After eating and much conversation, Michelle and Daniela clear the table. Daniela comes back into the dining room with a cake with 20 candles lit. Michelle turns the lights out and everyone sings happy birthday to Chutney. When she makes a wish and blows the candles out, Michelle turns the lights back on.

The cake has a picture of Chutney on it.

"What did you wish?" asks Reshawn.

"You are not supposed to tell anyone Reshawn or the wish doesn't come true," says Michelle.

"I don't mind I am not superstitious, Michelle. My wish is the same since I was nine. I want to be a Top Model," says Chutney.

Daniela cuts the cake and passes it around.

"I have something for you. I was going to wait until we got back to the hotel, but I guess now is as good a time as any," says Harrison as he pulls a box out of his pocket.

Chutney squeals with excitement. Michelle gets up from her chair and walks over to where Chutney is sitting so that she can get a better look at whatever is in the box.

Chutney unties the bow on the box and lifts the top to expose a pink Michael Kors watch with diamonds for numbers.

"Thanks Harrison, I love it," says Chutney as she reaches over to give him a kiss.

Reshawn frowns and says, "Yuck."

Everyone bursts into laughter then Savaughn says "yuck" too with a big smile.

After eating cake they all retreat to the living room and watch a movie then Harrison and Chutney decide it was time to call it a night.

When they arrive back at the hotel they settle into bed and quickly fall asleep.

(The next morning)

After having breakfast they decide to go and pick up Michelle, Reshawn and Savaughn to spend the day with them at the mall as well as show Harrison around the city.

When they arrive at Chutney's mother house the kids are already coming out of the door they are ready to go. Harrison makes sure they are all in their seats and buckled in while Chutney goes in to say Hello to her mother.

Chutney walks into the living room where she sees her mother tying her shoes as she is getting ready for work. Today she has to be at the hotel where she is in charge of housekeeping.

"Hey Mom," says Chutney as she walks over and gives her mother a hug and a kiss.

"Hey baby, what time are you going to have them back?" asks Daniela.

"What time do you get off?" asks Chutney.

"At five, but tomorrow I asked for it off since you leave so early on Monday morning," says Daniela.

"Okay I will have them back by 5:30 then," says Chutney.

"Okay well I will see you then, Chutney, do you really like this man?" asks Daniela.

"Yeah, he makes me happy and he buys me the nicest things," says Chutney with a smile as she admires the watch on her wrist.

"That's not what I asked you dear," says Daniela with a raised eyebrow.

"Mom he is the nicest man I have ever met. He respects me, he pulls out chairs for me and he cares about how I feel," says Chutney.

"I just see the way he looks at you and I know he cares a great deal for you. I know how vain you are and when I saw him it made me question the relationship. Be careful of what you wish for and besides my mother always said you want a man that loves you more than you love him. That way he will never leave you," says Daniela.

"Mom he does and he wants to take care of me. Have you been getting the money that I have been sending you?" asked Chutney.

"Yes, thank you. I think he is a nice, friendly, and he has manners," says Daniela.

"A nice man with plenty of money that wants to take care of me," says Chutney.

"Okay well you guys have a great day, let me get to this job," says Daniela as she stands and grabs her keys and purse. They both go out the door.

When they get to the mall the kids are excited they walk around for awhile. The first store they go into is Macy's.

Once in there they make their rounds to just about all the departments: Men's, boy's, girls, kids and the women's section.

When they get to the counter Harrison pulls out his credit card and charges $1300.00 worth of clothes and shoes.

All three kids thank Harrison upon the advice of Chutney. They walk a little more they stop to watch a teen fashion show that was going on in the center of the mall.

A strange man walks up to Harrison and introduces himself.

"You are Harrison Allen of the L.A. Clippers aren't you?" asks the man.

"Yes, I am," says Harrison as he switches the bags he was carrying to his other hand and shakes the man hand.

"Baby I told you that was him," says the man.

"Can we get your autograph and a picture?" asks the woman as she walks closer to Harrison while pulling out her camera.

"Do you mind taking the picture Miss," says the man.

The woman hands the camera to Chutney with a big grin on her face.

"We are huge fans of yours, Mr. Allen," says the man.

Chutney takes the picture and hands the camera back to the woman.

"What brings you to Tennessee?" asks the man.

"I am visiting my girlfriend's family," says Harrison.

"Hope you have a nice stay, you will love Tennessee," says the happy couple as they walk away happy about seeing one their favorite basketball players in the mall.

"Is you famous?" asks Michelle.

"Are you famous," says Chutney, correcting Michelle's grammar.

"You can say that, I play basketball and people love the sport," says Harrison.

"Momma said you have a lot of money," says Michelle.

"Really, I don't have money like Oprah, but I guess I do okay," says Harrison with a smile.

"Okay I want to go into Baker's shoes," says Chutney trying to change the conversation.

They all go in and Harrison purchases two pairs of shoes for Chutney then they all go to the Food Court.

Chutney treats everyone to lunch including Harrison.

They walk around a little more then they leave the mall because while at the Food Court a few more people recognized Harrison and it was beginning to be a bit much how they were crowded around their table wanting autographs and pictures with the star athlete.

When they get back to the car Chutney drives because she wants to take Harrison by her old high school, the park where she used to hang out at and where her grandfather lived. It is now just an empty lot across from a Church's Chicken, where she ate many times while visiting her grandfather's house.

After sightseeing they return to Daniela's house. Harrison is feeling good about spending time with the kids and Chutney, he liked her family. The kids asked a lot of questions, but he did not think anything of it, that's just something kids do.

Daniela is home when they arrive. She is relaxing on the couch with the television on.

"Hey guys did you have a good time with Harrison and Chutney?" asks Daniela then she observes all the bags that they are bringing into the house.

"Yes," says the kids in unison.

Michelle takes her bag and dumps it out on the couch.

"Ms. Daniela I bought the kids a few things I hope that it is okay," says Harrison.

Daniela is speechless.

"Did you guys say thank you?" asks Daniela.

"Yes, momma they did. They had a good time and they had lunch at the mall," says Chutney.

"You guys take all that stuff upstairs to your rooms and I will look at everything later. I am going to start dinner," says Daniela as she grunts to get up off the couch.

"Ms. Daniela I had plans of taking you all out to dinner tonight. Why don't you get dressed and you can choose the restaurant. My treat," says Harrison.

"You don't have to do that," says Daniela.

"I want to. You cooked a nice meal the other night and I wanted to return the favor," says Harrison.

"Come on Momma, go and get dressed," says Chutney.

"Babe let's go and get showered, change and come back," says Harrison.

"How about we meet you at the restaurant, I want to go to Red Lobster," says Daniela.

"Mom you can do better than that. I'll choose the restaurant, I'll call you when we get back to the hotel," says Chutney.

Chutney and Harrison get up to leave, but not before Chutney informs the kids that she will see them a little later that they are all going out to dinner.

"Can I go with you?" asks Michelle.

Chutney looks back at Harrison and he nods his head, "Yes."

"Go get your stuff," says Chutney and Michelle takes off to her room to gather her belongings.

When they get to the hotel Chutney immediately orders Michelle to take a bath.

Chutney and Harrison go into the bedroom and begin to decide what they were going to wear to dinner.

When Michelle comes out of the shower Chutney goes in and makes sure it is clean before Harrison goes in to take his shower. Once Harrison has closed the door and in the shower Michelle asks Chutney to put 2-3 braids in her hair, something that Chutney often did before she left home.

Michelle looks nice in the clothes that Harrison had purchased for her a pair of True Religion jeans, True Religion T-shirt and a new pair of Michael Jordan tennis shoes.

"Chutney, I want to go back to L.A. with you, I hate it here all I do is babysit all the time," says Michelle in a desperate voice.

"I know because that is all I did. Mom was always gone to work one of her two jobs. Michelle I cannot take care of you, you're only 13 years old. When I left I was older," says Chutney.

"Chutney he is not cute, you always have a cute boyfriend," says Michelle.

"Lower your voice. I know, but he is nice to me and watch your mouth, remember who bought you those clothes you got on," says Chutney.

"When I saw him yesterday for the first time I thought your real boyfriend was hiding somewhere," says Michelle.

They both burst into laughter.

"Michelle he is nice and besides he has a lot of money, which is always good. You better get used to him being around because I like him. I know he ain't cute, but he pays the bills," says Chutney.

Just when Chutney was finishing braiding Michelle's hair Harrison was coming out of the shower and they changed the subject of their conversation.

 They finished getting dressed and went to the restaurant.

They met at Ruth Chris Steak House, a restaurant that Daniela always wanted to go, but never had the funds to pay for it.

When the waitress brings their dinner to the table Harrison blesses the food and everyone starts to dig in.

"Chutney what are you going to do now that the Charity is up and running," asked Daniela.

"I am working there, did I tell you my face is on the pamphlets and that I did a public service announcement commercial too," informs Chutney.

"No, you did not. I am so proud of you," says Daniela.

"Chutney when are you going to do another rap video?" asked Michelle.

"Never," says Chutney and she shoots Michelle a mean look.

"You did a music video?" asked Harrison in shock.

"That was a long time ago," stammers Chutney.

"No it wasn't," says Michelle under her breath.

"How long ago," says Harrison as he looks at Michelle.

"Like a year and a half ago," says Chutney as she looks down at her food.

"A lot of girls do videos while they are trying to get into the big time," says Daniela trying to smooth things over with a slight smile.

"Baby it was tasteful and yes I had my clothes on," says Chutney.

"What kind of clothes?" asks Harrison.

"Short shorts, heels and a tank top," says Chutney as she looks at Harrison.

"You got the video?" asks Harrison.

"Yes. It's at Mommy's house," informs Chutney.

"I wanna see this when we get back to your mom's house, please," asks Harrison.

"Sure, are you mad?" asks Chutney.

"No, but I don't want my girl on some video with all her stuff hanging out," says Harrison as he finishes his meal.

"I don't have everything hanging out. You'll see it was a guy I met when I first got to L.A. he is a rapper and asked me to do it for a measly $500.00 and I did. I was about to be on the street," says Chutney with tears welling up in her eyes.

"Baby don't worry about it I am sorry. You will never have to worry about that type of thing anymore. I am going to take care of you," says Harrison.

Daniela hands her daughter a napkin and Chutney wipes her eyes.

"That was before you I would never do anything to embarrass you," says Chutney.

"I know. It's okay, let's all just have a good time," says Harrison.

"Thanks for welcoming me into your home and your family Ms. Daniela. I have had a good time here this is my first time being in Tennessee," says Harrison.

"You arc welcome Harrison, anytime," says Daniela as she raises her glass of water and winks her eye at Harrison. She is very impressed by his chivalry.

They enjoy the rest of the evening and their meal when they leave dinner they go back to Daniela's house. Harrison reviews the music video and Chutney was right it was tasteful, though Harrison thought the outfit given to her to wear was a little skanky he did not hold it against her. It made him realize how hard life has been on her and the things people do for money.

Chapter Seventeen

It has been a week since they returned to L.A. after their Tennessee trip. Chutney got a call from Tammy that Christian Dior was looking for models and she should try-out for it, when she did the people from the Dior Agency loved her walk and body type and gave her the job on the spot the job pays $700.00 per day and they will be shooting for five days, Chutney was elated.

The first day of the shoot was hectic and long, but they assured her they got some really good shots. The photographer asked her where had she been all his life.

On the last day of the shoot it was in a park and Harrison decided to stop by and see how the shoot was going, but he did not tell Chutney that he would be there; he did not want to make her nervous.

When he heard the camera guy say it was a wrap and everyone began to clap he walked up to where he could get Chutney's attention and when he does she is surprised and happy to see him.

"Hey you look beautiful," says Harrison as he gives her a kiss on the forehead.

"What are you doing here? I thought you would be working out."

"I was, but now I am done and I wanted to see what my girlfriend was up to."

"She is working."

"I see."

"Chutney can you come here for a minute please?" asked Lisa, the director of the shoot.

"Sure, babe I'll be right back," says Chutney as she gives him a peck on the lips then she strolls over to the woman.

"I'll be in the car," says Harrison.

"Hey, I was noticing the guy you were talking to, is that Harrison Allen from the L.A. Clippers?" asked Lisa.

"Yes, as a matter of fact he is," says Chutney as she looks at Harrison walking to his car.

"Is that your boyfriend?" asked Lisa.

"Yes, why?" asks Chutney.

"I was just wondering. I am a fan of the Clippers and I am having a dinner party at my house later, would you guys like to come?" asked Lisa with a smile.

"I'd have to ask him, but sure I don't see why not," says Chutney.

"I will have my assistant give you the directions and your check and I'll see you at six," says Lisa.

"Sure," says Chutney as she walks away to go and change with a big smile on her face.

When Chutney gets in the car with Harrison as they are pulling away she tells him about the invitation to the dinner party that she is so excited to attend and Harrison agrees. She tells him to stop by the mall so that she can get an outfit for the evening.

(Later that evening)

When they arrive at the house it is beautiful and there is valet parking for the guests.

When they walked into the foyer they are greeted by staff waiters that hand them both a glass of champagne and wishes them a good evening. The aroma of food and fresh flowers fill the air.

Chutney falls in love with the double staircase and marble flooring. They walk into the room where they see the other twenty or so guest have gathered and there are waiters and waitresses walking around with platters of food and wine flutes filled with champagne and a man playing a Steinway piano.

The room has a huge fireplace, ice blue couches and loveseats with grey chairs, a chaise lounge and they can see a few more guests outside on the patio.

"Hello, welcome to my home," says Lisa as she extends her hand.

"Hi, Ms. Masters, thank you for inviting us. Harrison this is Ms. Masters, the Director of the shoot from today. Mrs. Masters this is Harrison Allen," says Chutney.

"Lisa please, that's my name when I am not working," says Lisa.

"Hello, nice to meet you," says Harrison with a smile.

"I am such a L.A. Clipper fan," says Lisa as she waves over a photographer she hired for the night.

"Can I have a picture please?" asks Lisa. she grabs Harrison and cuddles up to him for the picture as if they were BFF's..

"Sure," says Harrison as he sits his glass down on the mantle of the fireplace.

The three of them take a picture then Lisa asks if she can have one with just her and Harrison.

Lisa grabs Harrison and cuddles up to him for the picture as if they were BFF's. "Please make yourselves at home, dinner will be served in about ten minutes or so," says Lisa as she walks away to greet some of her other guest.

Lisa is a white woman whom looks to be in her late forties, but you can tell she has had a little Botox around the eyes and lips. She has long thick brown hair, petite figure and a gorgeous smile.

Harrison assumes she is single because she never said anything about a husband and all the pictures in the room are collectables or of her and a little white Maltese dog that later Chutney informs him she lovingly calls, "Girlfriend." Girlfriend was also on the shoot with her dog sitter, a gay male by the name of Gabe.

When it was time for dinner Harrison and Chutney were ushered out along with other guest to the outdoor patio area with a pool that had yellow votive candles floating in it.

The dinner table was set beautifully and they were served blackened salmon, greens, bread and an Italian salad. For dessert the guest were served a decadent white truffle triple layer cake with ice cream (if desired). As they feast on dinner they were all serenaded by a woman playing a harp softly by the pool.

At dinner Lisa made the announcement that Harrison of the L.A. Clippers was a special guest and had Harrison and Chutney sit at the head of the table by her.

After dinner a live band called Special Formula played as Chutney and Harrison enjoyed a glass of wine under the stars as some of the guest came over and introduced themselves to them as a few of them were fans of the Clippers and they were given invites to a few more upcoming parties that the guest themselves were having.

"Thanks for inviting me I am having a good time."

"You are welcome I am beginning to think I was only invited because of you."

"Chutney, Lisa is your friend."

"She is not. She only invited me when she saw me talking to you."

"She would have invited you anyway."

"No. She wouldn't have she had not spoken to me all day until she saw us talking."

"Well it doesn't matter because we are here now, are you having a good time?"

"Yes."

"Besides you are the prettiest woman here."

"That is true."

Without saying a word they clang their flutes together and burst into laughter.

Chapter Eighteen

It has been a few months and modeling jobs are pouring in for Chutney and Essence is on the way to the condominium to interview Harrison and he wants Chutney by his side.

Chutney is making more money modeling than ever and she is sending money back home regularly. Michelle is taking modeling classes that she desperately wanted, Daniela has bought new furniture and has paid off her car that she was upside down in the payments.

"Babe you ready?" asked Harrison.

"Yes, Nacara is finishing up my makeup now. I'll be in there in a minute." Just then the doorbell rang and Harrison still tying his tie walks to the door to open it.

"Hello, says Shameca, a writer for Essence whom would be conducting the interview followed by the camera crew.

"Hello, come on in."

"Where can we set up?" asks Shameca.

"I thought we could do the interview in my living room and maybe take a few shots in there," says Harrison as he leads then into his formal living room.

Chutney walks into the living room and introduces herself to Shameca and the rest of the camera crew.

Chutney has on a floor length off the shoulder blue dress, silver sandals, several silver bangle bracelets, diamond ear rings, her hair is flat ironed straight and her makeup has blue and silver hues.

"You are even more beautiful in person," states Shameca.

"Thank you," says Chutney as the two women embrace.

"Can I offer anyone something to drink?"

Everyone declines they are ready to begin the interview.

Harrison re-enters the room.

He is dressed in dark blue jeans, a white button down shirt with a tie with blue, silver and pale pink hues. It was clear they wanted to somewhat match for the photos.

The interview was going well until Shameca started to dig deeper into Harrison and Chutney's relationship.

"So people want to know how did you two meet?"

"I was at a club with some of my teammates and she happened to be in the same club."

"So was it love at first sight?"

Harrison and Chutney look at each other and smile.

"I don't think so, but I knew I had to see her again and we did and the rest is history." "Chutney where are you from?"

"I am from Tennessee."

"What brings you out to California?"

"Modeling."

"How long have you guys been dating?"

Harrison decides to answer that question.

"It's been a year and a half now."

"Now that you are a couple your face has been appearing in some big campaign ads such as Calvin Klein, Chanel and Hennessy ads. Do you attribute that to your relationship with Harrison because before that people had never heard of you?"

Before Chutney answers she is blind-sighted by the question she considers it a hit below the belt, but she clears her throat looks over at Harrison, smiles and answers the question.

"Well somewhat. I have done ad campaigns for the House of Dereon, JCPenney, Sears and Macy's just nothing as big as the work I am doing now."

"So dating Harrison the number one draft pick has had its benefits."

"Yes, it has, but I have also worked my butt off to get to where I am. Dating him has made me more visible, but I am the one who has to book the jobs."

Harrison clutches her hand and adds.

"She is an amazing model she can sell anything with this beautiful face."

After a few more questions they begin the photo shoot. They even take some of them in the bedroom where Chutney and Harrison are lying opposite of each other and looking into each other's eyes. The camera is positioned over them.

After the interview Chutney is a little annoyed by the questions that she was asked in regard to her modeling career and dating Harrison. Harrison assures her she would have been discovered anyway.

He tells her sometimes it is about who you know and that if she was not good at what she does it wouldn't matter anyway and to give herself credit for that and not worry about what people say.

They go to dinner to celebrate a successful interview and photo shoot, but in the back of Chutney's mind she is well aware that Harrison is the reason why she is getting work, but she has to prove herself to be deserving of the work. She knew she had what it took to make it, she just needed a break.

At dinner Harrison offers that she comes to live with him since she is there all the time anyway and Chutney accepts. He hands her the spare keys to his condo and places a generous kiss on her lips.

Chutney squeals with excitement.

"I am ready to go to the next level with our relationship and to let you know that I am serious about you. Chutney I love you."

"I love you too."

"I am sure Tammy will be glad that you are moving."

"Yes, I'm sure she will. I feel so lucky."

"I am the lucky one."

"Harrison you could be with anyone you want to and you chose me sometimes I think about that and I wonder why?

"Chutney you are beautiful and you have goals and dreams. You are a hard worker and you care about family. I don't know we just click I can be myself around you and there are no expectations of who I am suppose to be."

"What do you mean?"

"When I was with Bahari, everyone expected me to marry her, but when we got to college I don't know I started to see things different because for the first time I was away from my parents and everything I knew. I started to wonder if she really was the right one for me."

"Really I always thought that because you met me, you started having doubts."

"No, it was before you. Don't get me wrong I was very attracted to you and had no idea I would go from one relationship right into another, but it just happened and I am happy, you make me happy. I like that we come from different backgrounds. When I do something for you it seems you don't take it for granted, but Bahari was different she has had everything given to her on a silver platter either of us has never wanted for anything."

"Well I am appreciative no one has ever been so nice to me and did not demand something in return."

"Chutney I did love Bahari, I still do just in another way. I guess it just got to be boring to me it seemed my whole life was planned for me and I thought that was what I wanted, but in the end when I thought about it that was not what I wanted at all."

"Bahari is a lucky girl. She is rich, smart, she comes from a two parent home and she had a fine rich boyfriend as well. Me I grew up poor, I hated school and I never knew my father. Every man I have known has wanted something from me. That is why I had to get out of Tennessee, make something of myself and never look back."

"I was thinking I am still living in the condo I think we should go house hunting it is time to buy a grown-man house. My mom mentioned to me when she last visited that it was time to buy a house and since we are taking this thang to the next level let's find a house together."

"OMG are you for real. I would love that," says Chutney with a big smile on her face.

"I love to see you happy, with the season being over let's start looking as soon as possible."

"Okay," says Chutney as she gets up and gives Harrison a big kiss.

"When we get back to the condo I promise to make you happy and put a smile on your face," says Chutney as she returns to her seat with a devilish look on her face.

After they have dinner and return to Harrison's condo Chutney keeps her promise with a happy ending to the evening.

Chapter Nineteen

Harrison and Chutney are house hunting in the affluent area of Orange County they have seen several homes that they either can't agree on or they feel does not fit their lifestyle. They plan on having many parties, family gatherings on holidays and someday even raise a family there.

When they get out of the limousine with the realtor Chutney is in awe of the beautiful home that sits in front of her.

"This estate has 5 bedrooms and 5 baths, over 5,500 square feet, 3 car garage, an open floor plan and a load of other amenities. Shall we take a look inside?" asks Sarah the realtor.

"Babe I love it already," says Chutney as she grips Harrison's hands tighter.

Harrison smiles, but says nothing.

When Sarah opens the door to the mansion, Chutney and Harrison can see out to a massive patio with panoramic views of the coast, a sunken large living area that is beautifully decorated and a roaring fireplace that has been pre-lit for the awe effect. The home smells of fresh cut roses.

Sarah takes them into the gourmet chef kitchen that has three ovens, a six burner stove, steel appliances, a marbled center island that matches with the countertops, recess lighting with a bar that seats 8. The formal dining room features a large marbled table with 12 chairs and a crystal chandelier. Throughout the home there are high tray ceilings.

"You will have no excuse to cook now," says Harrison in a stern yet joking voice.

After looking at the other four bedrooms, office, powder rooms, game room and work-out rooms. Sarah saves the master suite for last.

The master suite has double doors and Harrison lets Chutney do the honors of opening them.

"They were both surprised at how expansive it was.

"This room is 1,000 square feet," says Sarah with a smile.

It has a beautiful king sized bed, fireplace, his and her closets, and a sitting area, a private balcony that overlooks the ocean that leads into an oversized bathroom with a separate shower and bathtub with a view of the ocean as well.

"Baby I love this house I can so see us living here," says Chutney as she gives him a hug.

"Me too, it is beautiful," says Harrison as he looks out into the ocean while holding Chutney in his arms.

"Well you haven't seen the rest of the house. There is a beautiful resort style backyard with everything you need for a backyard barbecue, let's go and check it out," says Sarah with a smile.

They go back downstairs and go onto the patio.

It is has a full kitchen and outside private bathroom with a built in grill, waterfall, fire pit, pool and spa. The main outdoor attraction was the hidden movie screen for movie night under the stars.

"This house has everything we need Sarah I can't question that, but I do question the price, how much?"asks Harrison with a serious look.

"Well with the housing market right now the asking price is 2.4 million, but I think we can get it for less than that because it has been on the market for awhile and I know the owners are anxious to sell. You want to make an offer?" asks Sarah as she is shuffling her Ipad and some other papers in her arms.

Harrison looks at Chutney.

"Can we have a moment please?" asks Harrison.

"Sure," says Sarah as she walks away and places a call.

Harrison turns to Chutney.

"Baby I love the house, do you really want it it's going to be a lot to clean," says Harrison with a smile.

"Clean, we will get a maid," says Chutney as she turns to look out at the view from where they are standing on the patio.

"Seriously shall we make an offer?" asks Harrison.

"Yes," says Chutney in a squeaky happy voice with a big smile.

Harrison kisses her deeply.

"I am so excited, we are actually doing this," says Harrison with a smile.

"I am so happy. Harrison a year ago I never would have thought that I would be living in a mansion, I was a waitress sleeping in my friend's guestroom and then you came into my life."

"Well you won't be doing that anymore you will be sleeping with me."

Sarah comes back onto the patio and catches them enthralled in a deep kiss.

"I guess that is a, yes, on making the owner's an offer. I think we should come in at 2 million," suggests Sarah.

"Sounds good to me, when can I expect to hear from you," asks Harrison.

"Give me 2 weeks could be sooner though," says Sarah.

"I just love this house it is incredible," says Chutney.

"You are a very lucky woman," informs Sarah.

"Thank you I am excited," says Chutney as she kisses Harrison on the cheek.

"Okay well I will give you a call as soon as I hear something," says Sarah.

Sarah locks up the house and waves them goodbye as Chutney and Harrison stand hand-in-hand and stare at the house.

"Baby I cannot believe that I am going to be living in this house. I have never even had my own room before."

"I am an only child so I wanted someone to share a room with."

"Believe me it can get on your nerves."

Harrison kisses her then they get into his car and leave. Chutney turns around in her seat to see the house disappear into the distance.

They go to lunch then to Harrison's condominium and make love.

Chapter Twenty

Chutney and Tammy are out to lunch, Chutney's treat.

"Wassup Chica, I have not seen you in awhile, I feel like I don't have a roommate anymore."

Chutney stands to give Tammy a kiss on the cheek.

"Actually you don't I am moving out."

"Shut up, you guys are moving in together."

"Yes, Tammy I am so happy, but guess what?"

"What."

"We are buying a house, it is gorgeous. The house is over 5,000 square feet, pool, spa, private gym, outdoor kitchen and everything."

"I am so happy for you and I been hearing you have been getting some good modeling jobs, too."

"Yes, and I may be doing a job for the L'Oreal campaign that is going to pay well and If I get it I will have to travel to New York for a few days."

The waiter comes and takes their drink orders. They both order chocolate martinis and shrimp salads.

"I told you modeling was going to happen you just had to be patient and look at you now."

"I know last year this time I was living in your guest room struggling to pay bills."

"I am going to miss you."

"You will have an open invitation. Tammy thanks for everything, you are the best friend a girl could have."

The waiter returns with their drinks.

"Let's make a toast, to friendship."

They clang their glasses together then take a sip.

"When can I see the house?"

"Soon we are waiting to hear from the realtor."

"Has he asked you to marry him yet?"

"No, but he will."

"I taught you better than that, if he wants you to live with him he needs to put a ring on it."

"He will."

"How do you know that? Has he talked marriage at all?"

"No, but he says things like he will always take care of me and I never have to worry about anything anymore."

"Okay, but that is not a ring honey."

The waiter returns with their salads.

Chutney was about to dig in until she saw Tammy bowing her head so she did too. Tammy blessed the food after a little silence.

"I am just trying to get you to see that you have to protect yourself. You are sex-ing him and living good right now he can put you on the street at anytime. Remember honey athletes can be real creeps. Have heard what happened to Porsha on the Housewives of Atlanta."

"I did, but Harrison is a gentlemen and he would never treat me that way."

"I am sure Porsha thought the same thing about Kordell now look at her she's living with her momma. You don't want that to happen to you. As a girlfriend you are entitled to nothing, as a wife you can get paid, shoot Porsha gets $5,000.00 a month in spousal support. She is crying a lot, but they don't show the smile on her face when that money hits her account."

They both burst into laughter.

"I see what you are saying."

"I guess you have gotten over the fact that he ain't no Morris Chestnut."

"Girl my little sister Michelle called him ugly."

Tammy laughs. Then Chutney joins her in laughter.

211

"What did you say?"

"I told you to lower her voice before he heard her and how sometimes you have to consider how a man treats you and that Harrison is good to me."

"Wow."

They both take a sip of their martinis and munch on their salads.

"I want you to talk to a friend of mine he is an attorney and he can guide you through this process. I will not live with a man I was not married to."

"People do it all the time."

"They do, but are they living with pro athletes? These women will do anything to get a pro athlete, but you already got him, he is whipped. The fact that he was a virgin, girl you hit the jackpot. That is rare for an athlete."

"He is and I know at times I am blinded by the things he buys and does for me, but there are times that I do feel some kind of way about him. I have never had a man to treat me so nice, Tammy I am going to keep him by any means necessary."

"As you should, shoot I am just glad that you are out of my guest room. I have always told you that you were beautiful."

Chutney looks at Tammy and smiles.

"Do you love him?"

"I don't know, but I love the way he takes care of me. He gave me a credit card the other day."

Chutney's cell phone rings.

"Hello."

"Hey baby."

"Really, I am so happy when can we move in?"

"Okay, I'll see you later."

"Okay."

"See you later, bye."

Chutney hangs up the phone.

"We got the house."

"I am so happy for you, but you need to get him to marry you."

"He will."

"How do you know that?"

"Because Harrison is a stand-up guy and he loves me."

"Don't be stupid. I see these guys do it all the time. They move women into their homes or buy them their own condos or apartments, take care of them and then when they get bored of them they put them out, cut them off financially and they are back to where they started from, broke."

"That is not going to happen to me I got this."

"Okay well you sound like a woman with a plan."

"I do."

"You still seeing Harrison's friend?"

"Yes sometimes. See that is what I am talking about, he just wants to f??? He is not looking for a relationship. He will buy me things, take me on trips, dinners and even pay a bill. He says he loves my independence, but he does not want to get married or be in a serious relationship right now. I found out he has a girl he loves in his hometown and they have been dating since they were teenagers. I will probably pick up the paper one day and see that he has gotten married.

"Close your legs to him then."

"I can't the love-making is crazy and he can eat some p???? Like nobody's business, I have got to get into some counseling to get over him."

"Girl you are so stupid."

The two friends slap hands and burst into laughter. "Did your mom like him?"

"Of course she did, but she lectured me on the fact that she felt I did not like him as much as he liked me."

"Harrison is the type of guy that a mother would love."

"He is just not as attractive as I would like a man to be, but he has everything else. I wish that maybe I wasn't a model and maybe his looks would not matter or maybe I am just vain."

"You are vain honey and ain't nothing wrong with that. Who doesn't want to snuggle up to a hottie."

"He has a nice body and he can dress his behind off. He is also generous and kind to me. His family is so close I just wish I had grown up in a family like that. I don't think his grandmother likes me too much."

"Grandma ain't no joke, huh."

"Girl, he and his grandmother are very close he really listens to her and goes to her for advice."

"What about his mother and father, do you like them?"

"Yes they are cool. After working on Harrison House with his mother we talked a lot and she just wants the best for him. His father was easy he seems to be a little quiet and so is his grandfather."

"Well hopefully he is not the type of man to let his family come in between you guys and he will make his own decisions."

"I think he will."

After eating the rest of their meal the women pay their bill and leave the restaurant.

When Chutney gets to her car she reflects on their conversation, but she doesn't care what anyone says she loves the lifestyle she has now and she vows to herself that she will not let anyone stand in her way.

Chapter Twenty One

Three months have passed and Chutney has worked tirelessly with an interior designer to get the house to look and feel like home for her and Harrison. Tonight she has a prepared a meal of steaks, baked potatoes and a salad, the first meal in her new outdoor kitchen.

"Babe the house looks great I love it. You know my mom is dying to get here to see it."

"I know and she will tomorrow I can't wait to hear what she thinks of the furniture and the paint colors."

"Don't worry she's gonna love it."

"I'm always nervous when your mother comes to visit."

"I know and that is why I told her to come when the house was finished so that you can do your thang."

"Thanks baby."

"You're welcome."

"I want to talk to you about something."

"What is it?"

"I went to the Doctor the other day and I am pregnant."

Harrison puts his fork down and stares at her.

"What?"

"I said I am pregnant."

Harrison stands to his feet and walks over to her and gets on his knees.

"Really you know this for sure, how far along are you?"

"Yes, I am 2 months."

"I am just glad that I did the job in New York already."

"What does this mean for your career?"

"Harrison of course I can't model and be pregnant."

"I know you will have to give that up, what do you think about that?"

"I want to know what you think about me being pregnant."

"Chutney I want whatever it is that you want. I am happy I love you. How do you feel?"

"I am happy, I just wished we were married first and besides what are your parents going to say?"

"I think they would be happy, but that would be a concern for them as well."

"Have you told your mom?"

"No I wanted to tell you first."

"I'm happy. Chutney I'm gonna be a dad, I promise I will always be there for you and take care of you."

Harrison kisses her passionately on the lips.

"I'm sorry this happened now."

"What are you sorry for you did not do this alone, we are in this together."

"Harrison you always make me feel better no matter what."

Chutney smiles at Harrison and they kiss deeply.

"Harrison can we call my mom now and tell her together?"

"Sure."

Chutney gets up and goes to the kitchen to retrieve her phone. She calls Daniela and puts her on speaker phone.

"Hello," says Daniela in a cheerful voice.

"Hey Ma! What are you doing?" asks Chutney.

"Cooking," says Daniela.

"Mom say hello to Harrison you are on speaker," says Chutney.

"Hi Harrison what's going on?" asks Daniela in a concerned voice.

"Hi Ms. Daniela we are calling to tell you that you are going to be a grandmother in about 7 months," says Harrison in a cheerful voice.

"What how did this happen?" asks Daniela sounding shocked by the news because she knows her daughter was on birth control.

"Mom when two people—," Daniela stops her short.

"I know how it happens, but how did this happen you were on birth control," states Daniela.

"I was but I was late taking them and sometimes I forgot," says Chutney.

"Well are you ready to be a mom you are just a baby yourself," says Daniela.

"Mom I am going to be a good mom and my baby will have a father," says Chutney. Harrison reaches over and gives her a kiss.

"Harrison what does your parents think about this?" asks Daniela.

"We have not told them yet," says Harrison after clearing his throat.

"Oh I see. When do you plan too?" asks Daniela in a concerned tone.

"They are coming out here tomorrow and then we will break the news to them," says Harrison.

"I thought y'all were calling to tell me about the house and instead y'all got bigger news, a baby. Chile your momma is gonna have a fit. What is the hurry?" says Daniela.

"I just found out myself Ms. Daniela a few minutes ago, but I love your daughter and I am going to make sure that she and the baby have all that they need and more," says Harrison in a serious tone as he hugs Chutney.

"Well I can't wait to see the house. We will have to wait until the summer Tennessee is a long way from California and besides I got to wait until these kids get out of school," says Daniela.

"When you are ready just let us know and we will send the tickets," says Harrison.

"Baby I am going to go inside, clear the dishes and clean up the kitchen," added Harrison.

"I was going to do that Harrison I am not helpless," says Chutney with a smile.

"I know that, but I will do it," says Harrison and he kisses her on the forehead and goes into the house carrying both of their plates.

"Chutney take me off speaker," demands Daniela.

Chutney hits the button and puts the phone up to her ear.

"Chutney what the hell is going on we have been talking and you have not said anything about a pregnancy," says Daniela.

"Mom I wanted it to be a surprise," says Chutney.

"Chutney cut the bull you are going to mess up the best thing to ever happen to you. Harrison is a nice boy I have been bragging to all my friends and now you go and pull this," says Daniela.

"Mom, mind your business I got this," says Chutney in a calm voice.

"Chutney this is the oldest trick in the book it is right up there with prostitution. You are being messy," says Daniela.

"Mom I love you, but I don't have to explain anything to you I told you I got this," says Chutney in a sharp tone.

"You ain't got nothing you don't have a ring you guys are only living together, Chutney," says Daniela.

"Mom he will marry me watch and see," says Chutney.

"I said the same thing with your dad and look where that got me," says Daniela.

"But I ain't you Momma," says Chutney in a sharp tone.

"Okay well do what you gotta do, I gotta go. Anything else?" says Daniela.

"No, talk to you later," says Chutney and they both release the line.

Chutney gets the remaining items off the table and takes it into the kitchen where Harrison is just finishing up the dishes.

"Your Mom didn't sound too excited."

"She is she was just surprised is all."

"Chutney I am surprised weren't you taking the pill?"

"Yes, but when I went to New York for those four days I forgot my pills and when I got back we made love and that had to be when I got pregnant."

"Oh why didn't you tell me that?"

"What are you saying Harrison, I did this deliberately?"

"No I am not. I was just wondering since you were on the pill."

"I am not trying to trap you Harrison if I have to I will raise this baby on my own."

Harrison stops wiping the countertops and walks over to Chutney who is now sitting at the island in the kitchen with tears in her eyes.

"Baby no we are going to do this together. I love you and I am happy I just wasn't expecting this now," says Harrison softly as he stares her directly in the eyes.

"But I don't want you to think I am trying to trap you or anything because I do love you Harrison you are the first man in my life to treat me like you care and you want the best for me."

"I do Chutney and I think you are the most beautiful woman I have ever met. You got me I am ready to settle down and be a husband and a father. Will you marry me?"

"Harrison are you serious?"

"As a heart attack."

"We just found out we are pregnant are you sure you want to?"

"Yes, why put off the inevitable I want my son to have my name and you too."

Chutney has a big smile on her face.

"You have not answered my question babe."

"Yes. Yes I will," says Chutney and she jumps off the barstool into his arms and they kiss.

"We need to do this soon before you get fat and the baby comes," says Harrison with a smile on his face.

"You would use the word fat."

"Let's just have a small intimate ceremony only close friends and family say in about 3-4 months."

"That's a lot of work to get done in such a short amount of time. How about we have the baby then she could be at our wedding too."

"Absolutely not," says Harrison in a stern voice.

"O-kay."

"Look I love you and I don't want to wait I am ready to get on with our lives and start a family."

"Okay let's do it."

"And stop saying she it is going to be a boy I can feel it."

"What makes you so sure?"

"I just know. He will be beautiful like his momma and athletic like his daddy."

"Harrison I am a little nervous about telling your parents and especially your grandmother."

"Don't be it's gonna be okay I am a grown man and if I am happy they are happy, so stop worrying."

Harrison gives Chutney a kiss on the forehead then lifts her chin up and gives her a kiss on the lips.

"Come on let's go into the theatre room and watch a movie."

After watching "A Simple Plan" they both retire to the bedroom where they make love and fall asleep in each other's arms.

Chapter Twenty Two

Harrison's family has arrived and they are all around the table enjoying the barbecue ribs and fried fish that Harrison has prepared along with a salad, Texas toast, baked beans and potato salad. Chutney seasoned the fish, but could not fry it due to her condition the smell was making her sick.

Chutney eats a forkful of potato salad and immediately starts to feel extremely nauseated when she swallows. She takes a sip of her tea and swallows hard.

"So Chutney the house is beautiful you have great taste," says Katina.

"Thank you," says Chutney with a smile.

Chutney is feeling like she is about to throw up.

"Please excuse me," says Chutney hurriedly as she pushes her seat back and immediately goes to the master suite to the bathroom and closes the door.

"What's wrong with her?" asks Gwenn.

"I don't know," says Harrison as he excuses himself from the table to go and check on Chutney.

Harrison is outside the bathroom door listening then knocks on it as he patiently waits for the door to open. He hears the toilet flush.

"Baby open the door," says Harrison in a soft voice.

The door opens.

Chutney opens the door slowly.

"I'm sorry babe, but all of a sudden I felt so sick on the stomach," says Chutney as she looks in the mirror and smoothes her hair back.

Harrison wets a washcloth with cool water and places it on her forehead. Chutney takes the cloth from him and wipes her face with it.

"Don't be sorry, are you alright?" asks Harrison as he looks at her with a look of worry on his face.

"I'm okay just a little nauseated. Your parents are probably wondering what is wrong with me," says Chutney as she splashes water on her face.

"We will explain when we go back downstairs," says Harrison as he gives her a hug.

"Harrison I am scared," says Chutney with a sad face.

"You have nothing to be scared of I love you and this is my decision. Our decision," says Harrison as he grabs her hand so that they may go back downstairs.

"Wait I need to put some more makeup on," says Chutney as she reaches for her makeup bag.

She touches up her makeup and they go back downstairs hand-in-hand.

"Everything okay son?" asks Harrison's Dad.

"Yes, I need to tell you all something," states Harrison.

"What is it son?" asks Katina.

Gwenn and Grandpa Devereaux have stopped eating with a concerned look on their faces.

"Mom and Dad Chutney and I are going to have a baby and we want to get married before the baby comes," says Harrison as he clutches Chutney's hand.

"Son, how long have you known about this?" asks Mr. Allen.

"I found out yesterday," says Harrison.

"Are you ready for this? You guys just bought the house and trying to get settled in. You don't think this is moving fast?" asks Katina.

"Mom it is happening and I want to do the right thing by Chutney," says Harrison.

"I told you this was going to happen," says Gwenn as she throws her fork on the table.

"Grandma please," says Harrison.

"I told you this girl is after your money Harrison and you are too in love to see it," says Gwenn in an angry tone.

"Grandma we love each other and we want to be together," says Harrison.

"Is the child yours?" asks Gwenn.

"Grandmother I respect you, but you have respect me and my decisions and you are out of line for that comment," says Harrison.

Chutney bursts into tears and runs upstairs.

Harrison let's her go, but he is very upset.

"Sit down son," asks Mr. Allen.

"Dad I don't want to sit down I want to go and see about Chutney," says Harrison as he looks toward the staircase.

"I will go and check on her," says Katina with a worried look on her face.

Mr. Allen points to the seat next to him at the table.

"Son do you really love this girl?" asks Mr. Allen.

"I do. I was a little shocked by the news myself, but I want to be with her," says Harrison with tears in his eyes.

"I think she is a gold digger and I knew she would pull something like this. I had doubts about her from day one. I don't trust girls like her," says Gwenn.

Grandpa Devereaux places his hand over his wife's hand on the table and pats it for her to calm down.

"You don't have to marry her to be a father," says Mr. Allen.

"I know dad, but I want to. She makes me happy," says Harrison.

"When is the baby due?" asks Grandpa Devereaux. "In seven months," replies Harrison.

"Dad I just want to do the right thing. I want to have a family and give my son what I had with you and mom," says Harrison.

"But Harrison she is NOT the right one. Women have been getting pregnant by rich men for centuries it is\s the oldest trick in the book," says Gwenn in a defiant voice.

"Grandma I love her and I want this baby," says Harrison.

"Have you thought about abortion?" asks Gwenn.

"Grandma, NO I have not. We are happy and if you can't be happy for me, please keep it to yourself," says Harrison as he looks over at his grandmother.

"Harrison I will not have you speak to your grandmother like that. She is concerned for your well being. I have to admit this is awfully quick," says Mr. Allen.

"How long have you known this girl?" asks Grandpa Devereaux in a matter-of-fact tone.

"Almost two years," says Harrison.

"You are grown and you can do whatever you want there is nothing any of us can do about it," says Mr. Allen.

(Meanwhile upstairs in the master suite)

"How are you feeling?" asks Katina as she makes big circles on Chutney's back.

Chutney is crying lying across the bed.

"Mrs. Katina I did not mean for this to happen," says Chutney in tears.

"Sit up dear," asks Katina.

Chutney turns over and sits on the side of the bed next to Katina.

"Were you on the pill?" asks Katina as she gives her a hug.

"I am or was, but when I had that model shoot in New York I forgot my pills and when I got back things happened. I was not trying to trap him," says Chutney as she wipes her tears.

Katina reaches on the nightstand and hands her some tissue.

"Do you want to have the baby?" asks Katina.

"Yes ma'am. I love Harrison and we want this baby. I know the timing is bad, but we want to get married," says Chutney.

"Have you told your mother yet?" asks Katina.

"Yes we told her yesterday," says Chutney.

"What did she say?" replied Katina.

"She was shocked just like you," says Chutney as she blows her nose.

"Has the pregnancy been confirmed by a doctor?" asks Katina.

"Yes I went to the doctor already and I am 2 months," says Chutney.

Katina reaches over and embraces her.

"Well there is nothing we can do at this point, just take care of yourself and keep your doctor's appointments," says Katina.

"I don't want you and your family to be mad at me," says Chutney.

"We are just surprised by the news, but you know I have always wondered about a grandchild and if this is what you guys want to do I give you guys my blessing," says Katina.

"Really," says Chutney as she looks up at Katina.

"Yes and now I am going to have a grandbaby and a daughter," says Katina as she kisses the top of Chutney's head.

"Thank you Mrs. Katina. I want my baby to be raised in a good family and give him a father, something I never had," says Chutney.

"It is going to be okay, now we got to get Momma onboard because she has always looked at Harrison as her own she loves that boy. She is more protective of him than me and his dad. She is like a lioness protecting her cub," says Katina with a smile.

"She just doesn't like me," says Chutney with her head hung.

"Chile she didn't like my husband either when she met him it took her 3 years. She only softened when I got pregnant with Harrison and she saw what a good father and husband he was," says Katina.

"Really, I want her to like me," says Chutney.

"It is going to take time and patience, but I am sure she will when she sees that baby she will melt," says Katina.

"Thank you Mrs. Katina, you have always been so nice to me," says Katina.

"You will see when you have your baby that you just want the best for him/her and as long as your baby is happy you are happy. That comes along with being a mother," says Katina.

Chutney smiles at her and goes into the bathroom to wipe her face.

When she comes out of the bathroom the two women go downstairs and join the rest of the family.

After more talk about the baby and the upcoming wedding Grandma Gwenn still is unhappy about the news she went to her room without finishing the rest of her meal. Everyone else is trying to digest it and make the best of it.

The Allen's and Grandpa Devereaux welcome Chutney into their family and they all assure her that she will come around and that she will apologize for her outburst, Grandpa Devereaux said he would be talking to her in private about it.

The rest of the evening was quiet.

Chapter Twenty Three

The game is over and the team is in the locker room. Harrison is excited because he can go home after being away for more than a week from Chutney.

The locker room is alive with chatter, laughter and the sounds of hands slapping to celebrate the win against the opposing team.

Harrison is getting dressed when his cell phone rings and it is Chutney congratulating him.

"Hey baby, how r u feeling? And my little man?"

"Okay great. I will be home in about four hours. I love you."

"Okay see you soon."

"Bye."

Harrison hits the end button on his phone.

"Is everything okay?" asks Terry.

"Yeah man, just can't wait to get back home," says Harrison.

"So things are going good for you guys huh?" asks Terry.

"Yes. She is pregnant," says Harrison.

"Pregnant," says Chris in a surprised voice.

"Man, what are you going to do?" asks Terry.

"What do you mean? I love her and we are going to get married. I want to do it before the baby is born," informs Harrison.

"Whoa cowboy, you are moving a little fast. I had my reservations when you moved her into your home, but this is serious," says Chris.

"Man Chris is right. These women get pregnant to get a check for the next eighteen years and then they are on to the next player," says Terry.

"She is not like that, we love each other and we are going to get married and have this baby," says Harrison in a stern voice.

"Man you don't have a lot of experience with women. Wasn't she living with your girl Tammy, Terry?" asks Chris.

"Yes. She was a struggling model, sleeping in her guest room and broke. Tammy used to tell me how she sometimes didn't have money for her rent," says Terry.

"Man you bout to get taken for a ride. That chick was looking for a duck (sugar daddy) and she found one in you. You are a rich kid that sees the good in everybody, but you gone learn," says Chris with a giggle.

Before anybody knows what has happened Harrison has jumped on him and has Chris down on the floor and punching him vigorously in the face several times before they are pulled apart.

The Coach comes over and wants an explanation for the fight.

"Coach we good ain't nothing, it's under control, too much testosterone," says Terry with a smile.

"Yeah, coach we are good," says Chris as he wipes the blood from his nose.

"Harrison you okay?" asks the Coach in a stern voice.

"Yeah, I'm fine," says Harrison as he jerks away from Terrance, whom was holding him back. Harrison walks away, but not before punching a locker.

"Stop playing around and get ready to get on the bus ladies," says the Coach as he walks away.

"What was that all about," asks Terrance in a concerned voice.

"Remember the chic that was at the club with Harrison the night we took him out? Well he has plans to marry her," informs Terry in a low voice.

"I didn't know he was still seeing her like that," says Terrance.

"Yeah, we'll they live together and she is pregnant," says Terry.

"You bull???Me. I thought he was smarter than that," says Terrance.

"Dumb mofo I was just trying to help him," says Chris as he finishes getting dressed.

"Does he know if the baby is his?" asks Terrance.

"Man we don't know nothing more than what Terry just told you," says Chris.

"That's deep. Another one bites the dust," says Terry in a sad tone.

They all burst into laughter.

Harrison walks past them to get onto the bus and shoots them a nasty look.

(Later when Harrison gets home)

Harrison sits his bags down by the door and calls out for Chutney, but he hears nothing.

He goes into the Master bedroom and there she is fast asleep with the television on. Harrison stands over her and watches her sleep for awhile before waking her.

Harrison gently moves her long curly tendrils out of her face and kisses her.

He whispers in her ear, "Hi Princess."

Chutney rolls over barely opens her eyes and smiles.

"Hey Baby, I missed you."

"I missed you too."

They kiss passionately. Chutney sits up in bed as Harrison sits down on the bed beside her.

He places his hand on her tummy.

"How are you feeling?"

"I have been so nauseated I couldn't get anything done today."

"Is that a bad sign is there something wrong with the baby?"

"My mom says that some women just have morning sickness that lasts virtually all day. I tried to eat something and I threw it up so I pulled myself together enough to run to the store for some ginger ale and crackers that she recommended."

"Did you feel better?"

"A little I can't even drink a glass of water babe or I will throw up."

"Is there something I can do?"

"No not unless you are going to have the baby for us."

"Other than that what can I do?"

"I'm just glad that you are here now. I have been feeling awful for the last two days."

"Well I am home now and I will take care of you at least for the next three days."

"I wish I didn't fall asleep I wanted to put some make-up on I look terrible."

"No, you don't. You look beautiful as always."

"Thanks baby, but I know you are lying."

Harrison reaches to give her a hug.

After their embrace Chutney reaches for both of Harrison's hands.

She looks him in the eyes and says, "I want this baby to be healthy and happy."

Then she notices that Harrison hand is injured.

"What happened to your hand, babe?"

"I hurt it playing ball."

"Looks like you punched something, your knuckles are swollen. Come into the bathroom and let me put some peroxide on it."

"Chutney, don't make a big deal out of it. I play ball, I have bumps and bruises from time to time."

"Well I don't like it, so come into the bathroom and let me take care of it."

Chutney gets off the bed and escorts him into the bathroom, cleans the abrasion with peroxide then she puts a band-aid on it.

"Are you hungry?"

"No. I ate something earlier, just glad to be home."

Harrison stares at Chutney without saying a word.

"What's wrong why are you looking at me like that?"

"Chutney I love you so much. You have made me so happy and I want you to be my wife and the mother of my child. Do you love me?"

"Harrison what's wrong?"

"Nothing I have had a little time to think and I want to make sure I am making the right decision. I want you to be pregnant because you love me and I want you to want to be my wife because you love me. Do you love me?"

Chutney gives him a hug and lays her head on his chest. Harrison is looking at the two of them in the mirror waiting for her answer.

"Harrison I do love you. Who have you been talking to?"

"Nobody, I just want to be sure that's all."

Chutney looks up at him and hugs him tightly around his waist.

"Baby I love you so much, I am giving up my career to have this baby, but if you are having second thoughts I will raise him or her on my own. My mother did it with me, so I am sure I can do it too."

Chutney walks back into the bedroom with tears in her eyes.

Harrison turns the bathroom light off and follows her.

"Baby you won't have to be a single mom because I am not going anywhere. I only want to get married once in my life."

"Me too Harrison, but I don't need you second guessing me."

"I'm sorry, just forget about it."

Harrison helps her up off the bed, holds her in his arms and kisses her on the forehead.

"You are my princess. I love you and that is all that matters, Mrs. Chutney Allen."

Chutney looks at him with a smile on her face.

Now get into bed, let me get these clothes off and I will join you."

"Okay."

When Harrison gets in the bed he tries to forget about what happened in the locker room and assures himself that Chutney is the "One" for him.

Chutney knows that there is something that Harrison is not telling her. She also knows that he did not get that injury to his hand while playing ball. She is convinced he was in a fight of some sort.

After a few kisses Chutney massages his back until he falls asleep, Chutney soon follows suit.

Chapter Twenty Four

Chutney is at L.A.'s Fashion week an event she has always wanted to attend. She is there to support Tammy.

She has taken her seat when the lights go down and the pulsating beat of "Beneath Your Beautiful" by Labrinth ft. Emeli Sande when the first model hits the runway in a beautiful green and brown flowing gown.

After about three models Chutney sees Tammy strut her stuff down the runway in a Javan Reed original in a way that she demands that every eye is on her. When she gets to the end she gives the crowd a wink. It was perfect how she did it with a sly smile.

The show was awesome Chutney bought a few of the designs even though she is almost four months pregnant. After the show she goes backstage to congratulate Tammy.

When she gets back stage she sees Terry holding an armful of pink roses and an expensive bottle of champagne.

Tammy comes out of the dressing room looking like a million bucks.

"Hey baby!" says Tammy when she sees Terry.

"These are for you," says Terry as he gives her a quick kiss on the lips and hands her the roses.

"Hey," squeals Tammy as she gives Chutney a hug.

"Hey I was so proud of you up there. You looked amazing," says Chutney with a big smile.

"Thanks," says Tammy while smelling her beautiful roses.

"Baby can you put these in the dressing room I have to walk around a little bit and meet with some of the designers and buyers.

"Sure," says Terry with a smile and he takes the roses out of her arms.

When Terry walks away the two women talk. Several people are walking past and congratulating Tammy.

"So how have you been, or should I say mommy?" asks Tammy with a smile as she smoothes her hair back then touches Chutney's tummy.

"I am fine, but this retching all day has my energy level low, but I was not going to miss this event. Harrison has something to take care of so he could not make it. He sends his blessing," says Chutney.

Terry returns to the group and puts his arm around Tammy's waist.

"I'm glad to see you," says Tammy and she gives Chutney a hug.

"Are you going to find out what sex the baby is?" asks Tammy.

"No we want it to be a surprise," informs Chutney as she places her hand on her barely bulging tummy.

"Harrison wants a boy like all men do," says Terry.

"He is already saying it is a boy. He went as far as to buy a small basketball home the other day," tells Chutney.

"Where is he anyway?" asks Terry.

"He said he had something to do and he would meet us at the after party," says Chutney.

"I am going to have to leave you two for a moment I have to circulate," says Tammy with a smile because she sees Mr. Reed waving her over to a crowd of people he is talking to.

"Sure, babe you go do your thang. I am going to get the roses and champagne and take them to the car and I will meet you out front," elects Terry.

"Chutney I'll see you at the after-party and you look great," says Terry as he gives her a hug.

"Thank you Terry," says Chutney as she watches him walk away.

"He is something fine and a cutie too, that Tammy is a lucky women," says Chutney under her breath as she goes to the restroom she is feeling a little pressure and she is having cramps.

When she gets into the stall and uses the restroom she hears something fall into the toilet that is red in color shaped about half the size of a grapefruit and there is blood. Chutney is panicking.

She reaches for her cell phone and calls Tammy to come and get her out of the restroom, but she does not answer her phone. She is probably still making her rounds with the designers, she thinks to herself.

She calls Harrison panicked and sweating.

"Hello," says Harrison.

"Baby I am in the bathroom at the show and something has gone terribly wrong."

"What are you okay?"

"Harrison I am so scared there is blood everywhere."

"Oh My God I am on my way, just hang in there baby, I'm coming right now," says Harrison as he leaves the store in a rush.

"Baby, call Terry he is here and I can't reach Tammy because she is on the floor with the designers."

"Okay, I'll call him right now."

Harrison hangs up the phone and calls Terry.

"Terry where are you, man you got to get into the bathroom and get Chutney I think something is horribly wrong."

"I am out front waiting on Tammy."

Terry leaves the car parked on the street and runs back into the building straight to security.

"I have a friend in the restroom and something is wrong," says Terry in a panic to the woman security officer.

The woman gets on her walkie-talkie and calls for back-up and an ambulance.

They both rush into the ladies room, but by then the restroom is crowded with onlookers as two women are with Chutney trying to keep her calm. They are on the floor and there is a pool of blood surrounding Chutney. One of the women is a nurse and has the situation under control she has already called for an ambulance.

"Terry, help me!" says Chutney when she looks up and sees Terry.

"Help is on the way, try to stay calm," says Terry as he reaches down to try and comfort her.

"Where is Tammy?" asks Chutney sweating profusely.

Terry's phone rings just as the paramedics are entering the restroom therefore he gets out of the way.

One of the EMT's is a female and asks Chutney what happened.

"I am almost four months pregnant, when I went to the restroom I passed something in the toilet and when I looked there was blood everywhere," says Chutney.

"Is it still in the toilet," asks the female paramedic.

"Yes, I ask that no one flush it because I knew the hospital would need the fetus to examine it," says the female that was an off duty nurse.

"Thank you," says the male paramedic and he went into the stall and retrieved it.

"Which hospital are you taking her to, this is the father on the phone and he wants to meet us there," asks Terry in a panicked voice.

"Mt. Sinai, Sir," says the paramedic.

The paramedics put Chutney on the stretcher then Tammy runs into the restroom. "What is wrong with her," yells Tammy breathing hard in a state of shock after seeing all the blood on the floor.

"Calm down baby we are going to follow them in the car we are going to Mt. Sinai. Harrison already knows he is going to meet us there," says Terry as he is hugging Tammy and trying to calm her.

"Chutney hang in there we are right behind you," says Tammy.

Chutney just nods her head in agreement.

Terry and Tammy run out to the car and follow the ambulance to the hospital.

Upon arrival they see Harrison and he runs to the door where the paramedics are rolling Chutney into the ER.

"Baby I'm here," says Harrison as he grabs hold of Chutney's hand.

"Stand back Sir we have to take her upstairs for examination you can come up to the waiting room and I will come out to speak with you soon," says the ER Doctor.

Harrison kisses her forehead and they wheel her away.

Tammy and Terry are walking briskly up to Harrison. "Hey thanks man," says Harrison as the two men embrace briefly.

"She is going to be okay Harrison, we are here for the both of you," says Tammy with a worried look on her face.

"Thanks guys let's go up to the waiting room upstairs the Doctor says he will be out soon as they stabilize her to talk to me," says Harrison.

It seems like it had been hours, but in actuality it had only been about an hour and the doctor comes into the waiting area and calls out, "The family of Chutney Lawson."

Harrison, Tammy and Terry stand to their feet. The Doctor comes over.

"Is she your wife?" asks the Doctor with a sad look on his face as he takes his hat off his head.

"No she is my live-in girlfriend and I am the father of the baby," says Harrison.

"I am sorry to inform you that the fetus did not make it, she had a miscarriage," says the Doctor.

"What do you mean the fetus? It was a baby our baby," says Harrison in a loud rude tone of voice as tears roll down his face.

"Harrison come on he is just doing his job," says Terry in a somber voice.

Tammy immediately starts to cry.

"Job or no job, he was a baby," says Harrison and he breaks down crying. Terry is trying to hold him up and the doctor helps to literally carry him over to a chair where he just sobs aloud.

"When can we see her?" asks Tammy with tears streaming down her face.

"Soon, I will have a nurse come and let you know," says the Doctor. Then he turns to Harrison, pats him on his back and says, "I am so sorry for your loss."

Harrison just puts his hand up.

"Man you have got to pull yourself together, you got to be strong for Chutney," informs Terry with tears in his eyes.

Immediately Harrison sits up in his chair one of the ER nurses comes and hands Tammy a box of tissues and in turn she hands a few to Harrison.

"Man, Why?" asks Harrison.

"Man we don't question why it just wasn't the right time and GOD wanted his little angel back," replies Terry.

"I got to call my parents," says Harrison as he pulls his cell phone out of his pocket and he steps away from Terry and Tammy to make the call.

As soon as he returns to the waiting area the nurse tells them they can go in two at a time and visit with Chutney.

"She is in room 206," informs the nurse.

When Harrison reaches the door of her room he clears his throat, puts his arm around Tammy and opens the door.

Chutney is crying her eyes are swollen from the tears and she looks as if she has been through hell.

"Hey Baby," says Harrison with red eyes.

"Baby I am so sorry," says Chutney as she reaches for him.
"Baby no. You have nothing to be sorry for. I love you and I am here for you," says Harrison as they cry together for a moment.

"I am so sorry Chutney is there anything you need?" asks Tammy as she hugs her friend with tears in her eyes.

"No. I just want to be alone with Harrison right now. Can you call my mom and let her know what happened, but tell her I am resting and I will call her later," says Chutney then she bursts into tears.

Harrison hugs her and is kissing her forehead and cheeks.

"I will," says Tammy.

"Where is Terry I need to thank him," says Chutney.

"He is in the waiting room they would only let two of us in so he let Harrison and I come in," says Tammy.

"I want to see him," says Chutney.

"Okay I will leave and get him for you," says Tammy.

"Baby I love you," says Harrison.

Tammy comes around to the other side of the bed and gives Chutney a kiss and a hug goodbye.

After a few brief moments Terry walks in the door.

"You okay?" asks Terry in a soft voice.

"Thank you so much I don't know what I would have done had you not been there. Thank you so much," says Chutney crying profusely.

"It's okay, don't cry, just try to relax," says Terry as he gives her a hug.

Terry turns to Harrison.

"Man can I get you guys anything?" asks Terry.

"No," says Harrison with tears in his eyes.

"Hey, we gone get up outta hear, but if you need anything please don't hesitate to call," says Terry as he gives Harrison a long bear hug.

"Thanks man," says Harrison.

Terry says goodbye to Chutney and closes the door behind him.

Chutney turns on her side away from Harrison.

"Baby don't shut me out I am hurting too."

"Have you told your parents yet?" asks Chutney as tears roll down her face.

"Yes I talked to my mom and she is coming tomorrow," says Harrison in a somber tone.

"I guess your grandmother is happy now."

"Don't say that, now is not the time to entertain that. She will not be happy about this Chutney my grandmother is NOT a heartless woman."

"I'm sorry."

Harrison hugs her and they cry together once again as they embrace each other tightly.

The nurse comes in and advises that Harrison can stay, but Chutney needed her rest and she was going to give her a shot to help her sleep. After the nurse returns and gives Chutney the shot she turns the light off over the bed.

"Baby I will be right here when you wake up, I promise," says Harrison.

Harrison holds her hand until she falls asleep. As he watches her sleep, he cries and prays for her and grieves for the loss of his child. He takes the ring out of his pocket he bought earlier, looks at it and places the five carat ring on Chutney's finger and softly whispers, "Will you marry me." He was going to give it to her at the after-party for the fashion show.

Around seven o'clock in the morning Harrison hears Chutney waking from her sleep, but she is having a dream. He stands over her and shakes her because she is screaming.

"Baby I'm here."

"Harrison I was having a bad dream that we lost the baby," says Chutney as she begins to cry because as she looks around the room she remembers where she is and reality sets in that it is not a dream it was true.

"It's going to be okay," says Harrison as he hands her some tissue.

When she wipes her face and is about to blow her nose she notices the ring on her finger.

"Baby what is this?"

"It looks like a ring to me."

"I know that, but where did it come from."

"Me. Will you marry me Chutney?" says Harrison as he gets on one knee beside the bed.

"You still want to do this. Harrison I lost the baby," says Chutney as tears began to stream down her face.

"I don't care, I still want to marry you."

"I don't know Harrison," says Chutney as she admires the amazing ring on her finger.

"You don't love me anymore?"

"I do."

"So marry me then."

The nurse opens the door, but when she sees what is happening she steps out and silently closes the door.

"Yes, yes I will."

Harrison gets off his knees and they kiss passionately.

The nurse comes back in after about ten minutes.

"How are you feeling today?" says the nurse.

"I'm great, I'm getting married," says Chutney as she flashes the nurse the huge ring on her finger. The nurse looks at Harrison with a surprised look on her face.

"You are Harrison Allen right?" asks the nurse.

"Yes, this is the soon-to-be Mrs. Allen," says Harrison as he kisses Chutney on the forehead.

"I love basketball, I am a huge Clipper fan," says the nurse as she reaches for his hand to shake it.

"You are a lucky woman," says the nurse.

"I know," says Chutney with a big smile.

"I came to bring your discharge papers," says the nurse.

"She can come home today?" asks Harrison.

"Yes, not unless you want us to keep her," says the nurse with a smile.

"Oh, no I will take her home," says Harrison.

The nurse talks to Chutney about her medication and to make sure she follows up with her primary care doctor. Chutney is getting out of the bed and Harrison gets the bag that Tammy dropped off last night with Chutney a fresh change of clothes in it.

"I am going to get the car," says Harrison.

"Okay, we will wheel her down as soon as she gets dressed," says the nurse.

Harrison gives Chutney a kiss on the lips and walks out of the room.

"Do you know if the baby was a girl or a boy?" asks Chutney as she gets dressed.

"No, ma'am I don't. Honey you are young and you got a good man go home, get some rest, take care of yourself and try again. Don't look at what you lost look at what is ahead. Start planning your wedding honey," says the nurse in a loving tone.

"Oh yeah, I do have a wedding to plan. Thanks," says Chutney with a smile as she gives the older woman a hug.

"I am going to go and get a wheel chair," says the nurse with a smile.

Chutney gets her purse and tries to call her mother, but her phone is dead. She knows her mother is worried sick especially if Tammy has told her what happened to her yesterday.

The nurse comes back with a wheelchair, Chutney takes a seat in it. She is rolled outside to Harrison waiting for her in the car. Harrison helps her in the car, thanks the nurse and they drive off.

Chutney thinks back to what the nurse said about her being young, to look forward not look back and she was a lucky girl. Chutney smiles and grabs Harrison's hand for comfort and without saying a word to each other they smile at each other and head home to plan a wedding.

Chapter Twenty Five

It is the morning of the wedding and Chutney is getting her makeup done by Alisha of Beaten Faces when Tammy her matron of Honor walks in the door. Chutney has had a talk with Grandmother Gwenn last night at the dinner and they have made their peace. Grandma Gwenn is now walking around getting on the staff and making sure that everything is in order and that the food and flowers are in place. A job that Chutney thinks is best instead of her being in the room with her making her nervous.

"Hey everybody," shouts Tammy already dressed and make-up holding a bottle of wine.

"I am so glad you are here," says Chutney trying to keep still.

"Is there a bottle opener in here?" asks Tammy.

"No, but I will go and get one," says Daniela as she leaves the room.

"Mrs. Katina, this is my very good friend Tammy," says Chutney.

"Hi, I have heard a lot about you, sorry you couldn't make it to the bridal shower," says Katina as they hug.

"Duty called," says Tammy.

"You are more beautiful than your pictures I saw for the cognac ad in Essence magazine," says Mrs. Katina.

"Thank you that was so nice of you to say," says Tammy with a smile.

Daniela returns with a bottle opener and four champagne glasses from the kitchen. The wedding is being held in Harrison and Chutney's backyard. The house is decorated in yellow and brown.

Tammy takes it, opens the bottle and pours champagne in all four glasses.

"Mommy, this is Tammy you guys have talked on the phone, but never met," says Chutney.

"Hi Ms. Daniela, I thought you would have been tall," says Tammy then the two women hug.

"I thought that was you from the way you came into the room and have seen numerous pictures of you. You are simply stunning," says Daniela.

"Thank you," says Tammy as she takes a glass of champagne from Daniela. Then she passes glasses to Katina and Chutney.

"I want to toast to my friend whom has been more like a sister to me. I wish you health, wealth and lots of happiness," says Tammy with a raised glass.

All three women take a sip.

"Mom, Savaughn is running around like a crazy person and bothering things. Take him," says Michelle.

"Tammy this is my little sister Michelle, she is thirteen going on twenty-one," says Chutney with a smile.

"Hi," says Michelle.

Reshawn walks in the room.

"Michelle I got to use the bathroom," says Reshawn.

"And this is my little brother, Reshawn," says Chutney.

"Hi," says Reshawn as he looks at Tammy.

"I'll take you," says Mrs. Katina as she holds out her hand for Reshawn.

"I'll be right back," says Mrs. Katina.

As Katina walks out of the room Mrs. Johnson walks in.

Before Katina takes Reshawn to the restroom she introduces Mrs. Johnson to Chutney.

"Hello, you are such a beautiful bride," says Mrs. Johnson.

"Hi, nice to meet you, Harrison speaks highly of you and your family," says Chutney.

Mrs. Johnson gives her a hug.

"I am glad you guys could come and be a part of our special day," says Chutney.

Chutney stylist comes and puts the finishing touches on her hair by adding the flowers.

Tammy checks her watch.

"Is she ready for her dress, we got about fifteen minutes until show time," says Tammy.

Daniela takes the dress down which was hanging on the door and the photographer is ready to start taking pictures of Chutney as she slides into her beautiful Chocolate dress with a pale yellow belt.

Chutney stands.

"Where is Bahari I wanted to meet her before the wedding," asks Chutney with a confused look.

"She did not think it was appropriate for her to be in here, but she is here," says Mrs. Johnson.

"Oh," says Chutney as she walks over to her mom as Tammy and her mom helps her get into it.

"You can meet her at the reception," says Mrs. Johnson.

"I am going to go outside and grab me a seat. I will see you soon," says Mrs. Johnson as she gives Chutney a hug.

Mrs. Katina walks back into the room with Reshawn and Savaughn is on her hip.

"I'll see you outside, she is a lovely girl Katina," says Mrs. Johnson.

The two women hug.

(Meanwhile down the hall with the men)

"Dad can you help me with this tie," asks Harrison.

"Are you nervous," asks Mr. Allen as he starts to make a bow with Harrison's tie.

"A little," says Harrison.

"I am about to take care of that right now," says Terry as he hands Harrison a glass of champagne.

"Thanks for being my best man, Dad," says Harrison.

"Thank you I am so proud of you son," says Mr. Allen and when he is done tying his tie he gives his son a hug.

"We all are son," says Grandpa Devereaux and they do a group hug.

"Mr. Johnson I am glad that you and the family came because no matter what you, your wife and Bahari will always be myfamily.

"How is she?" asks Harrison.

"She is fine her and her mother are in there with the ladies I guess, thanks for inviting us," says Mr. Johnson.

"I was hoping to see Bahari last night at the dinner, but she did not come," says Harrison.

"I know and I wanted her to, but she declined saying she thought it would have complicated things for your bride, so she stayed at the hotel," informs Mr. Johnson.

"Maybe it was for the best. I'm just glad she came for the wedding," says Harrison.

"Bahari will always have a special place in my heart," says Harrison.

The room falls quiet.

"I want to have a toast," says Chris with a smile and a raised   glass.
"I haven't known you for long Harrison , but I know that you are a stand-up guy and a good friend with a helluva right hook, but all jokes aside I wish you happiness my friend and I'm glad it's you and not me," giggles Chris and he takes a sip of his champagne.

There is a knock at the door.

Terry opens the door and a beautiful woman with long brown hair, very curvy and a big smile with dimples asks to speak with Harrison.

"Your name please," asks Terry.

"Bahari."

"Harrison a young woman by the name of Bahari is here to see you.

Harrison has a surprised look on his face and he immediately looks at his dad.

Harrison goes to the door, walks out and closes it behind him.

"Hi," says Bahari.

"Hi," says Harrison with a smile on his face.

"I just wanted you to know I am happy for you and I am no longer angry with you. You are my oldest and dearest friend," says Bahari in a sincere tone.

"I am so glad you came though I did not think you would," says Harrison.

"I started not to, but I wanted to make peace with you it's been three years and we have both moved on," says Bahari.

"I am just sorry for everything," says Harrison.

"Let's just put this behind us, you look great," says Bahari.

"You do too. I have missed you being my friend," says Harrison.

"Me too, are you nervous?" asks Bahari.

"I was, but I am so much better now that I see you," says Harrison as he stretches his arms out with a big smile on his face.

Bahari looks at him, smiles drops her head and gives him a hug. They embrace and Harrison kisses her on the forehead. Bahari has tears in her eyes.

"Don't cry, we are good," says Harrison.

Harrison releases her from the hug.

"I am going to go and take my seat outside. I love the house by the way," says Bahari as she wipes her tears.

"Thanks for coming to talk to me Bahari it means a lot to me," says Harrison.

"I'm glad I did too," says Bahari as she walks away and doesn't look back because she knows that Harrison is watching her walk away.

Harrison's dad comes to the door and tells him it was time to go and take their places outside on the lawn.

Harrison goes in and grabs his jacket then all the men go outside and take their places.

The music starts then Reshawn and Michelle roll out the paper on the lawn for the bride to walk down.

Chutney appears on the arm of her Uncle Dexter looking stunning.

Every one stands and she begins to walk down the aisle.

When she takes Harrison hands he stares her in the eyes.

"I love you so much and you look amazing," whispers Harrison.

"Thank you and so do you," says Chutney.

After they exchange their vows and Harrison places her five carat wedding band on her finger Pastor Demetrus pronounces them "Man and Wife."

"You may now kiss your bride."

Bahari stands up with tears in her eyes and walks away. Everyone is looking at her, Mr. Johnson goes after her.

"Please turn to face your family and friends," announces the Pastor Demetrius.

"I know present to you Mr. and Mrs. Harrison Allen."

The crowd cheers loudly with claps and people saying their names.

Daniela has tears in her eyes.

Katina lays her head on her husband's shoulder with tears in her eyes.

Grandma Gwenn is quiet. She is still not happy with Harrison's choice in a wife, but she has agreed to disagree. She loves her grandson and family is more important.

After the wedding the bridal party is taking pictures and the guest have gone onto the patio and treated to finger foods and an open bar.

Tammy sees an opportunity to be nosey.

"Who was the female that got up and ran off then the man chased behind her," asks Tammy.

The other bridesmaids are looking also and waiting for her answer.

"She is Harrison's ex her name is Bahari I have not met her formally, just her mom, but I have seen pictures of her and she is actually prettier than I thought," says Chutney.

"Why is she here?" says Charlize, a friend of Chutney that she worked at the restaurant with.

"Harrison asked me if she could come because they have been friends since they were babies and it meant a lot to him. You know me I wanted to see what the ex looked like," replies Chutney with a smile.

"You are better than me because none of Terry's exes would come to my wedding, that is if he ever decided to marry me," says Tammy with a funny look on her face.

"Well that relationship is definitely over especially after today. He married the woman he wanted to be with so all that crying get the f??? outta here," says Chutney as she high-fives her friend Tammy.

"You think Harrison and her have been talking all this time?" asks Lisa another friend of Chutney from the restaurant and aspiring model.

"He says they have not he has not spoken to her since we got together, but he wanted to invite her and her family because they have been close all these years. His parents and hers still are very good friends," informs Chutney.

"What does she do for a living?" asks Tammy.

"She is in school to be a doctor at Duke University?" says Chutney.

"Oh, so she's a smart women too," says Lisa.

"I thought she was very pretty," says Charlize.

"That was her mother in the room the older lady with the long spiraled hair," says Chutney.

"I was wondering who she was because her and her husband came to the dinner last night too. They look like a nice older couple," says Lisa.

"They are both doctors. I was wondering if that was her hair. I hate fake womenes," says Chutney.

When they finally finish taking pictures they go to the other side of the lawn and enter the air conditioned tent where all of their guests are waiting for them. They have approximately seventy-five guest.

As the guest are just about finish eating Bahari sees her chance to have a word with Harrison's bride.

"Hello, I'm Bahari a friend of Harrison," says Bahari with her hand extended for a handshake.

The two women shake hands.

"Hi, I have heard a lot about you," says Chutney.

"Really, you area beautiful brideand it was a beautiful wedding," says Bahari.

"Thank you," says Chutney.

Tammy is watching the exchange.

"I love your home, did you decorate it yourself?" asks Bahari.

"I did with the help of a designer," says Chutney with a smile.

Harrison comes over to where the two women are standing.

"I see you two have met," says Harrison nervously.

"We have, she is beautiful Harrison I wish you both much happiness," says Bahari with a smile.

"Thanks Bahari that means a lot to me, I mean us," says Harrison nervously.

"How is school going?" asks Harrison also changing the subject.

"Good I start me residency soon and I am going back to Chicago?" says Bahari.

"Really?" asks Harrison.

"Toni is going to come with me," says Chutney.

"So you and Toni are still friends?" asks Harrison.

"Who is Toni?" asks Chutney.

"My roommate from school, yes we are and she wants to go as well. We have grown close like sisters, she sends her best wishes," says Bahari.

"Tell her I said thank you," says Harrison.

"I noticed you ran out on the wedding are you okay?" asks Chutney with a confident look as she holds onto Harrison tighter.

Bahari notices and swallows hard.

"Yes, well as you know we have history together and my emotions got the best of me," says Bahari.

"I am sorry to hear that, but the past is the past," says Chutney as she looks Bahari up and down with a slight grin and adds, "He is a wonderful man and one day a wonderful father to our children."

Bahari is silent then states sarcastically, "I know he's a great guy, remember I dated him too, we talked about having children together."

Chutney looks at her as if she wants to slap her.

Bahari looks at Chutney as if she were an alley cat.

"Uh Bahari, Chutney and I need to go and take more photos, glad you came," says Harrison as he grabs his bride's hand and whisks her off to stop the back and forth banter between the two women.

Chutney has a mean look on her face.

"I was okay with her being here, but you don't come to my wedding and insult me," says Chutney in an angry tone.

"Chutney you were both being juvenile," says Harrison.

"Me!" says Chutney in a high tone.

"Yes you. You started it by bringing up the fact that she ran out of the wedding you know her and I have history and that was wrong," says Harrison.

"Well I wanted her to know you are my man now," says Chutney with a sneaky look on her face.

"You think she didn't know that she is at our wedding babe, really," says Harrison.

"Well she needed to hear it from me, I claim what is mine," says Chutney.

"You did when you said I do. I don't want to talk about this anymore let's enjoy our day," says Harrison.

"You better not dance with her and I better not catch you talking to her or there is going to be smoke in the city," informs Chutney.

"You don't tell me whom I can talk to, but I won't dance with her," says Harrison.

Chutney shoots him a mean look.

"Baby don't act like that you are the woman I married. Let me see that beautiful smile of yours," says Harrison.

Chutney puts a smile on her face and agrees to put the incident behind them because after all she has the ring, the husband, the beautiful home and soon a beautiful baby.

When Harrison looks over to the table where his parents and the Johnson's are seated along with Bahari, she is hugging his father as if to say goodnight. Bahari grabs her purse off the table and walks toward where the cars are parked. He assumes she has left so that there are no more distractions. He knows Bahari hates confrontation and besides what they had is no longer. He wishes he could go after her, but he can't he just got married.

He hasn't thought about Bahari in years and now because he has seen her and she looks great like he knew she would, but those feelings for her were trying to come back. He will always love her.

The wedding planner is calling the newlyweds to the dance floor for their first dance. When Harrison pulls Chutney by the hand to the dance floor she is all smiles, but when he holds Chutney close he wonders what could have been with Bahari. He quickly puts those thoughts out of his head because he knows he scored big in getting such a beautiful, sexy and caring woman to marry him.

While dancing Harrison whispers in Chutney's ear to tell her that they will be cruising around the Caribbean in a chartered yacht with a private chef for a full two weeks for their honeymoon.

Chapter Twenty Six

It's been three weeks and Chutney and Harrison are back at home after a world wind tour of the Caribbeanand now real life begins. Harrison has left to go to Harrison House for a meeting with his staff and Chutney is waiting on Tammy they are meeting for lunch to give her all the juicy details of the honeymoon.

"Hey old married lady," says Tammy as she walks up behind Chutney sitting outside on the patio of Mr. Chow's.

"Hey."

"You look like you are glowing."

"Thank you that come from lying on that deck sunbathing all day."

"I am sure, I'm so jealous."

"I have never had a better time in my life and Harrison lavished me with a gift each and every morning everything from diamonds to bathing suits it was just amazing. I even got my own credit card."

"What, girl you give me hope."

"I brought you something."

"For me!"

Chutney takes a small box out of her purse and slides it across the table to her.

Tammy smiles and opens the box it is a pair of Tiffany diamond earrings.

"They are beautiful, but it's not my birthday."

"Tammy you gave me a place to stay when I could have been on the streets."

"Girl, you would have done the same for me."

"But you did not have to, I have never really had a good friend they all betrayed me in some sort of way and I just wanted to say thanks."

"You are welcome. I love the earrings."

"Didn't you tell me you had a friend that was an attorney?"

"I know two: My girlfriend Maya, a sports attorney and Marcus, remember the white older guy, he is a business attorney."

"That's the one I want, Marcus."

"You are getting a divorce already?"

"No silly, I just want to protect my investments."

"Women you ain't got no investments, Harrison has all the investments."

"WE have investments, I am his wife and I just want to make sure that we make sound investments."

"What are you talking about?"

"When we were on our honeymoon Harrison mentioned he wanted to buy a restaurant and I think it is a good idea, you know we love to eat."

"Wow, I wish Terry and I were a couple we could really get some things going. I want a shoe store slash boutique."

"Why do you keep messing with him and he won't give you what you want? I like Terry and I know he likes you. I asked Harrison about him when we were on our honeymoon and Harrison thinks that Terry is a commitment phobe as most professional male athletes are, especially the black ones."

"I knew that already."

"I noticed how attentive he was when I lost the baby and I couldn't help but think he is going to be a good father and husband."

"I noticed that too. I love him, Chutney. I date other guys, but he is the one that has my heart."

"Well don't rush it maybe he will come around, but don't wait on him."

"I don't, but even when I am with other guys I think about him."

"Awe. Well let's talk about the restaurant."

"Okay, do you guys have a name for it yet?"

"No. It will be an upscale seafood and steakhouse, but that is all we know for now."

"Look at you such the little business woman. I haven't wanted to ask, but are you guys trying to have another baby?"

"As a matter of fact we are I could be pregnant now."

"Really."

"Yes I just came back from my honeymoon. Harrison and I have been through a lot and losing the baby brought us even closer, he wants me to get pregnant we want a baby. Chile we were making love everywhere on that boat."

"Ooh sounds good. When we were living together you never wanted kids."

"Well I thought I was going to be modeling and I had no money to take care of a child, but being married to a millionaire gives me many options."

"I am sure it does."

After catching up on some gossip about other models, the industry and Tammy's last blind date the ladies pay their check and leave the restaurant vowing to see each other atleast once a month for lunch.

Chapter Twenty Seven

(6 months later)

Harrison has found a building for the restaurant and he and Chutney are expecting their first child, they are very happy. This time Harrison is scared to let her out of his sight he is making sure she eats right, he has hired a dietitian to cook during the pregnancy, he makes sure she gets enough exercise and rest. They are both excited she is four months pregnant.

The architect has some really good ideas for the build out because they will be gutting the old restaurant and building a new seven thousand square foot restaurant with a lounge area and a rooftop for parties.

It will take approximately a year for everything to come together, but they are happy about the dates because by then the baby will be seven months old.

"Marcus, the business attorney is acting as if we are spending his money."

"I like that he is cautious and wants us to stay within the budget."

"Harrison it is our money we can spend it however we want."

"I know, but I don't want to go broke either before we even get the doors open. Besides we have got to have ready cash because a restaurant is a tricky business we have got to be careful. Things are going to be a little tight for awhile because now we have payroll and not to mention a baby on the way."

"I know and a nursery to design. I talked to an artist to draw silhouettes of me you and the baby on the wall to do the story of the momma bear."

"How much Chutney?"

"$5,000.00

"That's a lot for a drawing on a wall."

"But it will be beautiful you will love it. Baby I am hungry, when are we going to get something to eat?"

Harrison looks at her, gives her a kiss and rubs her bulging belly.

"As soon as the contractors are done, are you going to be okay you know I have to leave for a few days?"

"I'll be fine without you fussing over me and I can eat whatever I want."

"I have given specific instructions for your diet when I leave young lady so don't give Mrs. Ann a problem while I'm gone."

"I won't daddy."

"I like it when you call me that."

"I know because you are nasty that is how I got in this situation in the first place."

"You were a willing participant."

"Why don't you see if your mom can come and visit?"

"She has to work, but she is coming for the birth of the baby."

"We are going to have a house full."

"Is your grandmother coming?"

"Yes of course to see her first great-grandchild are you kidding?"

"I just want her to like me. I thought your mother would be a problem, but she is cool. Your grandmother can be a bit much."

"I know she is just looking out for my best interest and she speaks her mind. She's old."

"Old or not when she comes to visit for the birth of the baby, please ask her to behave."

"Chutney this is my grandmother you are talking about."

"I would not allow my mother to disrespect you or anybody else for that matter."

"I do not allow her to disrespect you none of us has ever been able to control her mouth, not even my grandfather."

"Well if you won't I will."

"What does that mean?"

"You'll find out when she comes back into my house and thinks that she is running things."

"Chutney I am getting upset and now is not the time to have this conversation, because you will not disrespect my grandmother and that is the end of that. I will have a talk with her and I am sure everything will be fine."

"Okay, handle your business you have a family now."

"I am aware of that."

"Mr. Allen we will start the renovations on Thursday that is two days away I have your number so I will be in contact," says the contractor.

"Here are the keys."

"Thank you."

"Okay well I'll see you when you get back from your trip."

"Okay."

"Baby can we go and get something to eat now?"

"Sure let me check with the architect," says Harrison.

"Everything seems to be in order Mr. Allen this place is going to be awesome when you are done with it. Do you have a name for it yet?" asks the architect.

"As a matter of fact I do. It will be called Chutney's," says Harrison.

"That's a pretty name just like your wife," says the architect as he smiles at Chutney.

"Baby I did not know you were naming it after me I thought we were still trying to come up with names," says Chutney with a smile.

"I knew when I started this venture I wanted to surprise you," says Harrison.

Chutney walks over and kisses him passionately on the lips.

The architect just walks out the door leaving them kissing and closes the door behind himself.

"I love you."

"I love you, too."

They were not aware that the architect had left; they were caught up in the moment. They locked the door behind them and went to grab a bite to eat.

Chapter Twenty Eight

The day has come and Chutney is in labor she has dilated five centimeters. Daniela and Harrison's parents are at the hospital waiting for the arrival of Harrison if it is a boy or Hassa if it is a girl. Harrison's grandmother is at the house with Michelle, Savaughn and Reshawn. Harrison is pacing back and forth in the room.

"Son it is going to be awhile," says Mr. Allen.

"Dad she is in so much pain," says Harrison.

"Harrison I went through the same thing for you," says Katina.

"And it is hard to watch, but when I saw you it was the most beautiful day of my life," says Mr. Allen.

"Easy for you to say you weren't the one in all that pain. Chile I just wanted to get some rest," says Katina.

"Chutney came pretty fast when I got to the hospital I was ready to push," says Daniela.

"Mommy," says Chutney in a baby voice.

"I'm here honey," says Daniela as she wipes her forehead of the sweat.

Harrison walks over and takes her hand.

"Baby we are going to get through this together," says Harrison.

"It just hurts so badly. This pain is getting unreal," says Chutney as she grips hold of his hand.

There is a knock on the door and in walks the Doctor.

"Hello everyone," says The Doctor.

"Hi," says everyone in unison.

"Can I ask everyone to step into the hallway I have to check her she hasn't been checked since this morning," says the Doctor.

Everyone leaves the room except for Harrison and Daniela.

When the Doctor checks her he confirms that it could be any minute know, but he wants her water to break on its own.

"Can she have an epidural?" asks Daniela.

"We discussed this, are you her mother?" asks the Doctor before he gives her any information.

"Yes I am," says Daniela with a concerned look on her face.

"Mrs. Allen is that what you want?" asked the Doctor.

"I am trying to just hold on for now," says Chutney sweating profusely.

"Baby don't try to be brave if you want something for the pains please take it," says Harrison.

"I just want the baby to be healthy," says Chutney in a weak voice.

Just then Chutney feels like she is urinating and the bed is getting wet.

"Doctor, I think the baby is coming oh my god this pain is getting worse. Harrison please don't let go of my hand," shouts Chutney.

"I won't baby I am here," says Harrison.

The Doctor hits her button on the bed to call a nurse. The baby is coming.

After a few pushes Harrison Jr. is welcomed into the world.

Harrison is kissing Chutney all over her face the nurse brings the baby over for them to look at him. He has a very light complexion and silky black hair.

They nurse takes Harrison Jr. over to a table to be weighed and tagged with his name, weight and inches. After he is cleaned up they swaddle him in a clippers blanket that Grandma Gwenn made for him with a matching hat.

"Chutney he is perfect," says Katina.

Daniela is praising god for a healthy baby and that her daughter is okay.

Mr. Allen is taking photos of the baby with his camera.

"I can't believe I am a grandfather," says Mr. Allen.

"You I can't believe I am a grandma he is going to be so spoiled," says Katina.

"Can I hold him?" asks Daniela.

The nurse hands him to her.

"Baby, are you okay?" asks Harrison as the doctors are stitching her up.

"I am. Did you count his fingers and toes?" asks Chutney,

"I did, and they are all there," says Mrs. Katina.

"Baby he is the most beautiful baby I have ever seen," says Daniela.

"He sure is," says Mr. Allen.

"Can we take him back to Chicago?" says Mrs. Katina in a joking matter.

"He ain't going nowhere for a long time I got a lot of kissing and loving to do," says Chutney in a weak voice.

"Hey let's pop the champagne," says Harrison excitedly.

Mrs. Katina goes and gets it out of the ice bucket and Harrison passes out the glasses.

Mr. Allen is on the phone with Grandma Gwenn to give her the news that Harrison Jr. is here. He weighs 9lbs. 11oz., a head full of hair and healthy. Grandma Gwenn lets him know they are on the way to the hospital.

They make a toast, "Happy birthday to Harrison Jr. and thanks for the addition to our family Chutney we love you," says Mr. Allen with a huge smile on his face.

"Love you Chutney," says Daniela with tears in her .eyes.

Katina walks over and gives her a hug with tears in her eyes.

Chutney is so tired she can barely keep her eyes open she has been through a lot.

"Baby can you call Tammy for me and let her know I had the baby?" asks Chutney.

"Sure and I'll have her call Terry for me," says Harrison.

After making the call Harrison takes the baby in his arms and gives him a kiss.

"I love you little man, you mean the world to me," says Harrison in a soft voice.

Katina walks over and gives him a hug then his father joins them in a group hug.

"Daniela come and get in her you are family too," says Mr. Allen with his arms out to her.

As they embraced Katina said a prayer:

We pray for peace and that you have health and that you surpass the accomplishments of your parents as they look forward to the day when you are a strong successful man. We pray that you are kind, giving, be respectful to your parents and your family. You have been brought into a family of peace and love therefore you must carry it forward.

We wish for rest and healing for your mother this day and that she and your father teach you the way to GOD, manhood and to raise you properly in the way that GOD will have you go.

Peace my child. AMEN.

"Amen," they each say in unison and give each other hugs.

"That was beautiful, but we have to take the baby for some test then bring him back," says the female nurse with a smile. She gently takes the baby from Harrison, places him in the cubicle and rolls him out of the room.

"I miss him already," says Harrison says with a sad look on his face.

Harrison walks over to Chutney and kisses her passionately.

"I love you with all my heart thank you for this precious life, I will always be indebted to you my love," says Harrison with tears in his eyes.

The nurse comes in and gives Chutney a shot to make her sleep as the family is on the phone to family and friends to share the news of the birth of Harrison Jr.

Chutney looks at each of them with a smile on her face as she quickly drifts off to sleep.

Harrison spends the night at the hospital. He watches his son and his wife sleep all night as he feels a feeling of love that he has never felt before.

(3 days later)

Chutney is home Daniela, Harrison's parents and grandparents are at the house to help out with the baby.

Both she and Harrison are grateful for all the help that they are receiving and Harrison feels better leaving her home while he is on the road with the team he hated leaving her and the baby, but he had no choice.

Mrs. Allen comes into the room with some soup, a salad and a turkey sandwich on a tray.

"Thank you," says Chutney as she sits up in bed.

"You are welcome is there anything else I can do for you?" asks Katina.

"No. I just want to hold my baby and I want Harrison," says Chutney.

"I understand. I have given Harrison Jr. a bath already," says Katina.

"Where is he now?" asks Chutney.

"My mom has him she is giving him a bottle," says Katina.

"Can you bring him to me please?" asks Chutney.

"Sure right after mom burps him," says Katina.

"No, I want him now, please," says Chutney in a little firmer tone.

"Okay, I'll go and get him," says Katina with a weird look on her face.

Chutney's phone rings.

"Hello," says Chutney.

"What's up, I wanted to stop by today and see the baby. I just got back in town last night and I want to see you guys," says Tammy.

"Please can you hurry, these people are driving me crazy," says Chutney in a voice just above a whisper.

"Really, why?" asks Tammy.

"Girl they are trying to take over especially Harrison's grandmother. I don't like her and she doesn't like me," says Chutney.

"Did you want me to bring you anything?" asks Tammy.

Michelle walks into the bedroom and behind her comes Katina with Harrison in her arms and Grandma Gwenn carrying a bottle.

"No. I will see you soon," says Chutney.

The two say goodbye and they hang up.

Chutney squirts some sanitizer in her hands and then reaches for the baby.

"Hey baby, you smell so good," says Chutney.

"Thanks Mrs. Katina," says Chutney.

"He is so pretty," says Michelle as she sits beside the bed.

"I know right," says Chutney.

"He looks just like you," says Michelle.

Chutney looks at Michelle because her mouth is very unpredictable.

"Where is Mom?" asks Chutney.

"She is taking a nap, she was up late with the baby and she prepared breakfast," says Mrs. Katina.

"He sure is a greedy little something," says Grandma Gwenn as she sits the bottle down on the bedside table.

"And he can have as much as he wants," says Chutney in a baby voice as she kisses on baby Harrison.

"You can't over feed him his little tummy will burst," says Grandma Gwenn.

Chutney shoots her a mean look.

"I know how to take care of my baby," says Chutney.

"I did not say that," says Grandma Gwenn.

"Well what are you saying?" asks Chutney.

"Mom why don't you go downstairs and start preparing dinner," suggests Katina.

"When are you leaving?" asks Chutney.

"We will be leaving next week," says Mrs. Katina.

"No, I was asking your mother," says Chutney.

Grandma Gwenn stops in her tracks, turns around and shoots her a nasty look.

"I can be leaving tomorrow little lady. You are so disrespectful," says Grandma Gwenn.

"You have done nothing, but disrespect me from the day you met me. You cannot talk or treat me any kind of way. I am married to Harrison now like it or not," says Chutney as she hands Harrison to Michelle.

"Mom please I don't want this to get any messier than it already is," says Katina.

"She started it. I was trying to be nice and she takes everything I say and twist it around," says Grandma Gwenn.

"I know you don't like me, I know I am not your first choice for Harrison, but you are going to have to respect me in my house," says Chutney. "Mom please leave, I will come down and talk to you later," says Katina.

"Okay I am trying to be of some help to you while my grandson is away, I will stay out of your way," says Grandma Gwenn.

"Thank you, but it is clear we won't be the best of friends so let's stay out of each other's way," says Chutney.

Grandma Gwenn says nothing and walks out of the room.

"Please do not speak to my mother in that way again, being from the islands we respect our elders. I know Momma can be a handful at times, but she means well," says Katina.

"As long as she respects me I will respect her," says Chutney as she reaches for her baby from Michelle.

Mrs. Katina walks out of the room.

Chutney hears the doorbell ring and she assumes it is Tammy when she hears her voice she knows that it is.

"Michelle go downstairs and show her up," says Chutney as she straightens out the sheets and moves the tray of food to the other side of the bed that she has not touched.

Michelle gets up and goes downstairs and shortly afterwards Tammy and Michelle enter the room. Chutney is holding Harrison Jr.

"OMG he is so cute," says Tammy as she sits the armful of gifts she bought for the baby on the floor next to the bed,

"Hey girl, this is the new man in my life," says Chutney as she turns the baby so that Tammy can get a good look at him.

"Can I hold him?" asks Tammy.

"Sure. Get some hand sanitizer," says Michelle.

Michelle gets up and squirts some into Tammy's hand.

"She is being an overprotective Aunt, huh?" asks Tammy as she rubs the solution onto her hands.

"Yes, she tells me to use the sanitizer too," says Chutney.

"He is my baby, I love him," says Michelle in a loving tone.

"Awe and he loves you too," says Chutney as she gives her sister a hug.

Chutney hands the baby over to Tammy.

"He is so little and he smells so good," says Tammy.

"What do you have in this bag," says Chutney as she reaches down to get the bag that is filled with baby clothes and only GOD knows what else.

Chutney dumps the bag out onto the bed and a load of cute baby clothes fall out.

Michelle immediately starts to grab them and hold them up and so does Chutney.

Tammy has bought him eight outfits from church clothes, to play clothes and onesies.

"Thanks Tammy for everything," says Chutney.

The baby starts to fuss so Tammy hands the baby back to Chutney and she gives him a bottle.

Tammy watches while she gives him a bottle, burp him then lie him down on the bed next to her. After gossiping and a glass of wine, Tammy leaves so her friend can get some rest.

The rest of the day is uneventful she did not see Grandma Gwenn anymore that day. Mr. Allen and Grandpa Devereaux came into the room to hold the baby.

Chutney requested that the baby sleep in the bed with her because for the first night since she'd been home from the hospital she is going to get up with him to give Daniela, Grandma Gwenn and Katina a break. She has to get used to the late night feedings at some point.

Chapter Twenty Nine

It is the grand opening of "Chutney's" and the elite of Los Angeles has come out from Actors, Comedians, reality stars and athletes. Harrison and Chutney have hired an excellent executive chef from Louisiana. They hired John Paul as General Manager he has many years of experience in the U.S. and abroad and a wait staff that is impeccable.

They are booked with reservations. As the patrons dine on prawns, steak, salmon and other various fish and desserts they will be serenaded by Will Downing.

Downing will be performing in the main dining room.

The restaurant is a buzz and the food is coming out of the kitchen at a steady pace.

Chutney is looking beautiful in a beautiful dark blue, off the shoulder, tea length evening gown by designer Javan Reed of Jacksonville, Florida. Since she was introduced to his designs at the L.A. Fashion show she has been a fan every since.

Chutney is a little nervous she has not been away from Harrison Jr. since he was born. He is seven months old now and she still has a hard time leaving him with the nanny. Harrison is in the kitchen making sure everything is running smoothly. He is in a light blue crush velvet Versace suit, black tie and a white shirt.

Chutney is walking around greeting people and thanking them for being a part of their grand opening. Mrs. Katina is overlooking the lounge area where Mr. Allen is having a drink at the bar.

The restaurant is done in a mahogany wood with dark brown leather dinner chairs with white table clothes. The wait staff has on tuxedos, but in the lounge area the female servers wear tuxedo bodysuits and all the girls have the bodies of models and are very beautiful.

Chutney sees Tammy and Terry enter the front door.

"Hey," the two ladies squeal with excitement.

"Everything is so nice and girl it is filled to the gills in here. I am so proud of you guys," says Tammy.

"Thanks we have a sold out crowd tonight," says Chutney with a big smile.

"I see everybody who is anybody is up in here," says Terry as he gives Chutney a hug.

"You look great you do not look like a mother to a seven month old, you are wearing that dress," says Tammy.

"Thanks honey I had to hit the gym hard that baby fat ain't no joke," says Chutney as she grabs two menus.

"Come on I will take you to your table," says Chutney.

She stops at a table up front right in front of the band. She hands them the menus and tells them to have a good meal and that she'd be back a little later to check on them.

As she is walking away she feels a little woozy therefore she retreats to the kitchen for a glass of water. She tells John Paul, The General Manager that she is taking a break and she excuses herself.

When she pushes the door open, Harrison sees her and asks if she okay.

"Yeah I just feel a little hot and woozy," says Chutney.

"Maybe you are doing too much too soon I know it is busy out there, take a seat," says Harrison as he helps her to a seat.

"Babe I am okay. I just need to sit down for a minute," says Chutney.

The kitchen door opens and in walks Katina, she has just heard from John Paul that Chutney was not feeling well.

"What's wrong Chutney," says Mrs. Katina as she puts her arms around Chutney.

"I am going to get her a glass of water, I'll be right back," says Harrison with a worried look.

"I am fine I just need to sit down for a minute. Please don't make a fuss you know how Harrison is," says Chutney as she is fanning herself with her hands.

"Honey you may need to take it slow your body is still healing," says Katina.

"Mrs. Katina I want to be here and support my husband," says Chutney as her eyes fill with tears.

"Honey the baby is still young and this restaurant is going nowhere. I want you to take care of yourself," pleads Mrs. Katina.

Harrison returns with the glass of water and a napkin and hands it to Chutney.

Chutney takes a sip and blots her forehead with the napkin.

"Babe Dad is going to take you home. Tomorrow I want you to make an appointment with the doctor," says Harrison.

"I think that's a good idea, I am going to go back out on the floor and check on things," says Katina. She gives Chutney a kiss on the forehead, a hug and leaves the kitchen.

"Baby I don't want to leave. I want to stay here and support you," says Chutney.

"Baby I will be fine. We are a team whether you are here or not, I don't want anything to happen to you. Go home with the baby and I'll be there later," says Harrison with a worried look.

Harrison's dad comes into the kitchen.

"The car is out front, you okay?" asks Mr. Allen.

"Yes, your son is making me go home," says Chutney in an annoyed voice.

Harrison gives her a kiss on the lips and helps her to her feet.

Chutney stands to her feet, she still feels a little woozy, but she knows arguing with Harrison to stay is a fight she is going to lose. Chutney leaves the restaurant quietly.

Harrison is worried, but he knows he has to stay and close the restaurant, though he has a more than capable staff he wants to do it at least for the first time himself.

People are still flowing into the restaurant at a steady pace and the appetizers and dinners are coming out of the kitchen steadily.

Grandma Gwenn walks over to Harrison at the bar.

"Son this place is so nice," says Gwenn and Grandpa Devereaux agree with a nod of the head.

"I am glad you like it Grandma, did you guys eat yet?" asks Harrison.

"Yes and it was delicious, the couscous was prepared perfectly," says Grandma Gwenn.

"The grilled scallops in butter lemon sauce is awesome, Son we are so proud of you," says Grandpa Devereaux.

"Thank you," says Harrison looking around the room.

"Will Downing got these women in here falling in love all over again," says Grandpa Devereaux.

"Sure do. He was a great choice for opening night. We heard Chutney had to go home, is she okay?" asks Grandma Gwenn.

"I think she just needs some rest. She has a lot on her plate these days with the baby, taking care of the house and she helped design this place. She may be over doing it, but she is going to the doctor tomorrow nothing serious just to have a checkup," says Harrison.

"Her iron is probably low, no worries," says Grandma Gwenn.

"We are headed to the house anyway it is getting late we gone let you young folks have a good time," says Grandpa Devereaux.

Harrison gives them both a hug and his grandparents leave the restaurant.

Harrison sees many of his teammates in the restaurant, business associates and coaches he has a smile from ear to ear.

Tammy and Terry walk over to Harrison and congratulate him.

"Thanks guys, thanks for coming," says Harrison.

"Where is your beautiful wife she looks great she says she was coming back to check on us after seating us and she never did," says Terry.

"She had to go home, she was not feeling well," says Harrison.

"What do you mean? she was fine," says Tammy.

"I know, but she says she was feeling woozy and just to be on the safe side I sent her home, she is going for a checkup tomorrow. She will be fine. My Grandmother says her iron may be low," says Harrison.

"True, she did just have a baby and she has been pushing herself," says Tammy.

"She won't use the nanny like she should she is just so overprotective of Harrison Jr. that boy is going to be so spoiled," says Harrison and they all burst into laughter.

"Man the place is really nice and Will Downing is blowing the ladies minds he was a nice touch for the grand opening," says Terry.

"Thank you. Actually he was my mother's idea, you know me I would have had Marsha Ambrosius, Joe or Tank someone for the younger generation, but looking at the crowd she was right as usual," says Harrison.

"Chris came in a little earlier with two women on his arm, twins," says Harrison with a smile.

"Man you know how Chris do, he is wild as all get out," says Terry.

"Hey man we bout to get up outta here thanks for inviting us," says Terry as he gives his friend and teammate a hug.

Harrison hugs Tammy.

"I'll call and check on Chutney," says Tammy with a smile as they head for the door.

"Thank you, tell her I love her," says Harrison.

"I will," says Tammy.

Around two a.m. Harrison is closing the business and making his final draws from the registers and running the credit card receipts when his father walks through the door.

"Thanks for taking Chutney home," says Harrison.

"No problem, your mom says bring her some grilled scallops and linguine home," says Mr. Allen.

"Okay, Dad can you go to the kitchen and get it I have a lot to do here," says Harrison.

"Sure son," says Mr. Allen.

"Is there anything else you need from me?" asks John Paul.

"Just make sure both areas have been cleaned and the kitchen is in order," says Harrison.

"It's already taken care of. Is Mrs. Allen okay?" asks John Paul.

"Yes, she has just been doing too much she will be fine," says Harrison as he barely looks up from his paperwork.

"Okay well I will see you tomorrow and you enjoy the rest of your evening," says John Paul in his Italian accent.

"Good night," says Harrison.

Mr. Allen returns to the bar with his mom meal to go.

"Dad, take this key and lock the front door for me please," says Harrison as he hands his dad the key.

"Okay," says Mr. Allen.

"Mr. Allen the kitchen is cleaned and ready for tomorrow if there is not anything else I will be leaving now," says the executive chef.

"No. Thank you tonight was a success because of you and the rest of the staff. Goodnight," says Harrison.

"Thank you Sir," says the executive chef.

Harrison places the receipts inside his black book and closes it. He looks around and feels a feeling of accomplishment.

"Dad I couldn't have asked for a better night," says Harrison looking around the room with the look of pride on his face.

"Harrison you are such a man now I was looking at you tonight and it makes me proud," says Mr. Allen and he gives his son a hug and walks around the bar area.

"Let's have a toast, what can I get for you," says Mr. Allen.

"I'll have a bud light," says Harrison as he loosens his tie and relaxes in his seat.

"I'll have the same," says Mr. Allen.

"What do you think happened with Chutney?" asks Mr. Allen.

"Grandma thinks its low iron," says Harrison.

"Son, are you happy?" asks Mr. Allen.

"Yes Sir, I love being a husband and a father," says Harrison as his father hands him a beer and Mr. Allen comes from behind the bar to take a seat next to his son.

"Good it seems you have a bright future and a beautiful family. Chutney is looking fantastic," says Mr. Allen.

"She was determined to get back down to a size four," says Harrison.

"That's great that she cares about the way she looks these young women today they have one baby and look like they are the mother to six and have given up," says Mr. Allen.

"I know, but with Chutney being a model I don't think I have anything to worry about," says Harrison.

"Let's make a toast to family, business and a bright future for Chutney's," says Mr. Allen with his Bud light bottle elevated in the air.

After a few more beers, some jokes and his dad sharing with him how hard it was when he and his mother started out, they were ready to go home to their wives. Harrison locks up the building taking the bank bag to make the deposit in the morning.

The first night brought in nine thousand just in credit card receipts. Chutney's had a successful Grand Opening night.

(The next morning)

Chutney is in the bathroom getting ready to go to the Dr. for a checkup. Grandma Gwenn has the baby giving him a bath.

Katina knocks on the master bedroom door.

311

"Come in," shouts Chutney.

"Chutney I can take you to the Doctor," offers Mrs. Katina.

"No, my friend Tammy should be here any minute to take me, but thank you," says Chutney.

"Okay, when did Harrison leave?" asks Mrs. Katina.

"He is at the gym then he says he is going to the bank, he left around six this morning," informs Chutney.

Chutney hears the door bell ring, she puts a little lip gloss on her lips, grabs her purse and goes to open the door downstairs.

Katina retreats to her bedroom.

Chutney opens the door.

"You ready?" asks Tammy.

"Not yet, come in," says Chutney as she closes the door behind her.

Tammy and Chutney go into the kitchen where Grandma Gwenn is with Harrison Jr. giving him a bottle.

"I am off to the Doctor so that I can close Harrison's mouth and get back to work at the restaurant, but I couldn't leave without getting me some sugar," says Chutney as she reaches for Harrison Jr.

Grandma Gwenn hands him to her.

She kisses Harrison Jr. all over his face as Harrison Jr. is laughing. He is such a cheerful baby and he loves to play.

"Can I hold him?" asks Tammy.

"Sure," says Chutney and she hands him to her.

"How are you feeling this morning?" asks Grandma Gwenn.

"I feel fine, but I have to go to see the Doctor because Harrison says I can't come back to the restaurant until I have been cleared by the Doctor," says Chutney.

Chutney gives the baby another kiss and tell Tammy to give him back to his granny and they left for the Doctor's office.

(Meanwhile at the Doctor's office)

Chutney has been weighed, they have taken blood and urine and the Doctor is out of the room for a minute.

"Girl I wish they hurry up I am hungry," says Chutney looking irritated.

"Me too, that Doctor sure is fine. I wonder if he is married?" asks Tammy.

"I have no idea, he is cute though. I felt so uncomfortable with him all between my legs," says Chutney.

"Shoot he can get between mine," says Tammy with a grin.

"You so nasty," says Chutney.

The door opens and the Doctor comes back in.

"Mrs. Allen how are you feeling?" asks the Doctor.

"I feel fine," says Chutney as she sits up with the hospital gown on.

"Mrs. Allen you are three months pregnant," says the Doctor.

"What?" shouts Chutney.

"You haven't had any symptoms other than you feeling a little faint yesterday," asks the Doctor.

"No. I have been working out like crazy, my baby boy is only seven months pregnant," says Chutney.

"Well you will be having another in six months or so. Are you still having a period?" asks the Doctor.

"Yes, but it has been spotty I thought it was just because I just had a baby seven months ago and eventually it would regulate itself," says Chutney.

"Well it will probably stop soon. I will prescribe you some prenatal tablets and take it easy on the work out regiment. I want you to follow up with your OBGYN next month," says the Doctor.

"I can't believe this, I am not ready," says Chutney.

"You can get dress and congratulations Mrs. Allen," says the Doctor.

The Doctor smiles at her and leaves the room.

"Tammy I was not expecting this I love being a mother, but so soon," says Chutney with a look of disbelief.

"Harrison is going to be happy and so am I," says Tammy in a comforting tone.

"Tammy I don't want another baby right now maybe when Harrison Jr. gets about two years old. We just had the grand opening of the restaurant last night. I have a lot going on," says Chutney as she starts to put on her jogging outfit.

"You gone be alright and besides this could be a little girl," says Tammy.

"I know I wonder what Harrison is going to say," says Chutney.

"He's going to be happy," says Tammy.

After Chutney gets dressed and they get Chutney's prescription for the prenatal tablets they leave and go to lunch.

Chutney hopes that Harrison or better yet his Grandmother doesn't think that she got pregnant on purpose, because she is just as surprised. She will break the news to him tonight. Chutney is not ready for another baby she wants to prove herself in the restaurant business and maybe they can open another in the future. Having another baby so soon is going to complicate things.

Chapter Thirty

Chutney is five months pregnant and is slowly becoming quite the restaurateur, she has regular staff meetings, wine and menu tastings so that the staff can recommend the specials and they must be able to tell the patrons by memory how it is prepared.

Harrison is away at an away game. Chutney loved going to his games, but now with the baby and one on the way, the restaurant and Harrison House she has her hands full. She cannot attend every game.

Today Chutney has the nanny, Alicia and Harrison Jr. with her, she likes bringing Harrison Jr. when she has meetings, besides the staff loves him because he is friendly, cute and playful.

While the various companies are making their deliveries, the executive chef has prepared smoky cod and parsnip chowder, pan seared Chilean sea bass with citrus and pea tendrils filet Oscar, grilled vegetables, handmade herb and tomato pasta and herbal butter mash potatoes.

After explaining each dish and how it is prepared he hands a printed out sheet stating the same for them to memorize by the time that the restaurant opens at five p.m.

The executive chef leaves the dining area so that he may go and prep the dishes for tonight's dinner service. "So did everyone get a copy?" says Chutney as she stands to address the staff.

"Yes," as the wait staff respond in unison.

"Okay let's just go back over each of them one by one. Everyone please get a plate and we will start with the smoky cod," says Chutney. She loves the menu tastings because it gives her a chance to taste all the food on the menu, but more now because she is always hungry due to the pregnancy.

"This is really good," states Carl one of the servers.

"This is actually the special for tonight so please people let's do our best to sell this item on the menu," says Chutney in an authoritative voice.

After they discuss it and some of the staff members go back for seconds they move onto the Chilean bass.

"This is a delicate tasting fish and I like the bass, but in my opinion I am not crazy about the citrus and peas together not a favorite of mine," says Chutney.

"Mine either," says Cyndi another member of the staff that has Harrison Jr. on her lap.

It was not a favorite to most of the staff, but Chutney emphasis to them that dislike is an opinion and opinion is never to be shared with the patron especially if it is negative.

"Next we will be eating the File Oscar, which is a favorite of mine it is lightly seared on both sides and served with crabmeat drizzled with house made Béarnaise," says Chutney with a smile.

"This dish always does well on the menu especially with the men," says Mandy one of the more popular members of the wait staff she can sell salmon to a patron that says he does not eat fish.

"Mrs. Allen can I give the baby some of the mashed potatoes he is reaching for my food," says Cyndi.

"Sure, but just a little at a time," says Chutney.

"Ma'am I don't think that is a good idea," states Amanda the nanny.

"He will be fine," says Chutney in a stern voice.

Once they finish the tasting they move into the wine pairings for the dishes that they have just tasted.

"The feature wine tonight will be Chateau Climens the year is 1980," states Chutney as she pours each of the wait staff just enough for a sip.

Chutney does not partake in the wine tasting due to her condition.

"This is a white wine with a medium gold color, waxed with honey pineapple, delicate marmalade and citrus notes. It can be paired with the cod and the Chilean bass," says Chutney.

They each smell it, swirl it around in their wine glass, and let it rest on their palate then swallow.

Each of them agrees that they like it and some joked that they would like to have more.

Harrison Jr. is fussing to have a taste himself, but instead he is handed a bottle that he is now holding himself.

"The next wine that we will taste will be a Bertani Villa Arvedi Amarone 1999 is a dark powerful red wine loaded with black cherries, spices, menthol and minerals and is also strong on richness. This is a wine to be paired with beef such as the Filet Oscar," says Chutney.

"This is a little strong for my taste, but I am sure it will pair very well with the beef courses on the menu," says Mandel an oldest member of the staff.

"I wish I can have some, but as you all know my husband will have a fit," says Chutney as she rubs her stomach.

"Mrs. Allen how far along are you?" asks Cyndi.

"I am officially five months as of a week ago," announces Chutney.

"You wear pregnancy well I love this little one," says Cyndi as she looks down at Harrison Jr. as he sucks his bottle.

"Well if there are no more questions everyone get to work and I will be back a little later, any problems take them to Mandel and he will consult with me. This meeting is adjourned," says Chutney with a smile.

The wait staff gets up from the table and starts to clear it.

"Alicia, can you get Harrison? I would like to have a word with you," asks Chutney.

"Yes ma'am," says Alicia with a smile as she walks over to Cyndi to take the baby.

When the wait staff clears the table Chutney decides to have a word with Alicia.

"Did you forget who you work for?" asks Chutney in a sarcastic tone.

"No ma'am is there a problem?" asks Alicia.

"There is when you tell me what my baby cannot have and especially undermining my authority in front of my staff," says Chutney.

"Ma'am that was not my intention it's just that----," says Alicia as she was interrupted.

"If you want to keep your job when I say something or give you a direct order it is not up for discussion. Harrison Jr. is my child and I decide what is best for him, not you," says Chutney as she walks closer to Alicia, but at the same time trying to keep her voice down.

Alicia drops her head.

"Yes ma'am I was just making a suggestion," says Alicia.

"Unless I ask you for your suggestions don't volunteer them," says Chutney as she stands closer to Alicia.

"Hand me my baby," says Chutney in a sharp tone.

Alicia hands Harrison Jr. to Chutney.

"Learn how to keep your mouth shut and do your job, this is not the first time you have offered your suggestion like the time in front of my husband and he thought your idea was better. I should have fired you then," says Chutney as she walks away to go to the car.

Alicia says nothing she pushes the stroller behind Chutney and they leave the restaurant.

When they get home Chutney directs Alicia to give Harrison Jr. his lunch and put him down for a nap.

Chutney retreats to the master suite to take a nice long hot bath then take a nap before she has to get back to the restaurant for tonight's service.

When she gets into bed the phone rings.

"Hello," says Chutney.

"Hey baby, how are things going?" asks Harrison.

"I'm just a little tired I was about to take a nap to get ready for tonight," says Chutney.

"How is my little man?" asks Harrison.

"He is fine I ask Alicia to put him down for a nap. He went to the restaurant with me and he wanted to eat everything," says Chutney with a giggle.

"That boy has an appetite we gone need to open another restaurant just to be able to feed him," says Harrison.

"Babe, I think I may have to let Alicia go," says Chutney in a serious tone.

"What for did she do something to the baby?" asks Harrison in a curious tone.

"No she would be dead if she did something crazy, she is always undermining my authority," says Chutney.

"What do you mean?" asks Harrison.

"Today I told her to do something and she refused then she was talking back to me. I don't have time for that I have a lot going on with the baby and the restaurant," says Chutney.

"Well when are you going to have time to look for another nanny," says Harrison.

"Well I was thinking to have your mother come and do the interviewing for me she always have Harrison Jr.'s best interest at heart," says Chutney.

"Why don't I just have my grandmother come she would love to spend some time with him," says Harrison.

"No babe, you know her and I don't get along, she gets on my last nerve I don't want to be walking around in my house on eggshells and besides she cooks all that heavy food and you know I can't resist it. I don't want to blow up like I did with Harrison Jr.," says Chutney.

"This would be a good time for the two of you to bury the hatchet especially with the new baby coming," says Harrison.

"Harrison please don't do this to me, I don't need her here can we just call your mom," says Chutney.

"Can you just do it for me, I don't want my grandmother to feel she is not a part of my children's life, she loves taking care of Harrison Jr." says Harrison.

"This is emotional blackmail," says Chutney.

"Please I want you guys to get along, I heard about what happened when we had Harrison Jr. and I had to leave," says Harrison.

"Who told you?" asks Chutney.

"That's not important. Watch and see once you get to know her you guys will be the best of friends," says Harrison.

"I doubt that," says Chutney under her breathe.

"What?" asks Harrison.

"Nothing if that's what you want that's fine, but this time I want a white older nanny. I told you that before," says Chutney.

"Why?" asks Harrison."

"Because white people mind their business, do as they are told and they are not lazy. I have seen the way Alicia looks at you, she wants my man, my baby and my life," says Chutney.

"Babe come on really," says Harrison.

"You have to meet me half way on some things," says Chutney.

"Okay fine, can she be from the islands I think that would be even better and that way he can learn my culture," says Harrison.

"Well we might as well get a Puerto Rican nanny because that is part my culture," says Chutney in a smart tone.

"Baby that is fine I will call my grandmother tonight and hopefully she can be there by the weekend," says Harrison.

"Okay fine. I love you," says Chutney.

"I love you too, always," says Harrison.

"Bring me a win home baby," says Chutney.

"I will. Take care of yourself," says Harrison.

"Let me know when Gwenn is coming so I can get the guest room ready," says Chutney.

"Okay and thanks please try to get along with her," says Harrison.

"I will, I will keep Alicia on until I hear back from you," says Chutney.

"Okay and please pay her for an extra two weeks we want to look good for the agency we got her from just in case we need to use them again," says Harrison.

"I will," says Chutney.

"Get some rest I will call you later," says Harrison in a seductive tone.

"Please I like our late night phone calls. I miss you so much when you are not here," says Chutney.

"I miss you guys too, but someone has to make the money," says Harrison.

"I know right," says Chutney while giggling.

"Bye, baby," says Harrison.

"Bye," says Chutney as she hits the end button on her cell phone.

She lies down and thinks about the Alicia situation. "That women will learn that I am in control I almost snapped when she talked back in front of my staff and Grandmother Gwenn had better stay out of my way because this time Mrs. Katina ain't gonna be here to save her ass," Chutney says aloud to herself.

She pulls the covers up and goes to sleep.

Chapter Thirty One

(Skip ahead four months)

The baby has arrived it is a girl and the proud parents name her Hassa she has a head full of curly hair and pecan tan skin. She weighs 9lbs. 13oz. She looks identical to her brother when he was a newborn.

Mommy and baby are fine and at home resting.

"Mom being a parent is one of the best feelings in the world," says Harrison.

"It is and it is a privilege GOD has smiled on you son in many ways," says Gwenn.

Grandma Gwenn has been in Los Angeles for the last four months because Alicia has been fired, Chutney has not begun to look for a replacement. The relationship between Gwenn and Chutney it is cordial at this time. Chutney was glad that Mrs. Katina came and organized a party for Harrison Jr.'s 1st birthday, because she was so big at the time, she did not want to be bothered with screaming children. He loved it though he fell asleep before the party was over.

Chutney, Harrison and Harrison Jr. had their own little party when Harrison returned home after an away game.

Harrison Jr. is curious about this little person whom has invaded his space. Each time she cries he yells for his mother to come and see about the baby then goes into the room and gets a diaper. He thinks every time Hassa cries she needs to be changed.

Daniela is so proud of her grandchildren and they can do no wrong in her eyes.

Michelle is once again over protective and she is even happier that is a girl.

"Harrison Jr. is such an active child I wonder if Hassa is going to be the same way, if so you guys got something on your hands," says Grandma Gwenn.

"Momma don't say that Harrison Jr. is a handful he is curious about everything and is all over the place," says Mrs. Katina.

"She is going to be a little lady, I know for sure she is going to be a daddy's girl because already Harrison hates to put her down I keep telling him he is spoiling her," says Daniela with a smile.

"Ain't nothing wrong with dat more little girls need to be spoiled by their daddy's," says Grandma Gwenn.

"You right about that, she ain't gone want for nothing," says Harrison with a smile.

"I am glad that my grandchildren have a good father and my daughter has a good husband. My heart just sings every time I come here and witness the love Harrison has for his family," says Daniela as she kisses Harrison Jr. as he sits on her lap.

"Thank you I told you in the beginning that I would take care of your daughter, I love her," says Harrison as he kisses the baby on her forehead.

"I am going upstairs to check on Chutney she may be up from her nap," says Katina.

"Okay, thanks," says Harrison as he cuddles Hassa.

"Son, you gone let anybody else hold her," says Mr. Allen.

"He don't let nobody hold Hassa, her mom barely holds her," says Grandma Gwenn.

"I am I that bad? It's just that she is so precious and pretty," says Harrison as he smiles down at his baby girl.

"Hand her over," says Mr. Allen as he stands over his son with his arms stretched out.

"I guess I will hold her next," says Grandpa Devereaux.

"I'll just get in line, but until then I am going to love and kiss on this one," says Daniela as she tickles Harrison Jr. and he squeals and giggles.

"We have got to get a sitter for both the kids grandma can't stay here forever. I am going to call the agency tomorrow and have them send us some candidates for a new nanny," says Harrison.

"Yeah because I am missing my wife and my meals," says Grandpa Devereaux.

"Your sistah not coming over, we agreed that she would cook and bring it to you," says Grandma Gwenn with a surprised look on her face.

"She does, but I want to eat your food and I ain't got nobody to watch me television wit," says Grandpa Devereaux.

"Ah hush old man, Harrison is going to get a sitta and as soon as he does I am coming home," says Grandma Gwenn with a smile.

"I'm not complaining I am just messin' wit the old lady makin' her feel wanted ya know," says Grandpa Devereaux.

Harrison looks at the both of them and smiles he knows he wants to be them in about thirty years.

"Grandma, why you never had any more kids?" asks Harrison.

"Well I was thirty-eight when I had your momma and I guess GOD did not see fit that I had more. We were late bloomers," says Grandma Gwenn.

"Grandpa you never wanted a son?" asks Harrison.

"I did and I got one, your father many years later," says Grandpa Devereaux.

"Growing up I always wanted a sister or maybe even a brother. I want my kids to have each other," says Harrison.

"So do you guys want more kids?" asks Daniela.

"Yes I can see us having one more maybe just not anytime soon. Having these two are like having twins because they are only ten months apart," says Harrison.

Katina comes back downstairs.

"Chutney wants you to come upstairs," says Katina.

"Okay," says Harrison and he stands to go upstairs.

"Is my sister up?" asks Michelle.

"Yes, but let Harrison go up and when he comes down, you can visit with your sister," says Daniela.

"Okay," says Michelle in a low voice.

Katina smiles at her.

"You want to help me in the kitchen?" asks Katina.

"Yes, I might as well. Can we make some plantains and curry chicken?" asks Michelle.

"Sure," says Katina.

Katina and Michelle leave the den area and go into the kitchen.

"I'll be in there in a minute, I want to start a load of clothes first" says Grandma Gwenn.

(Meanwhile in the master suite upstairs)

"Hey baby," says Chutney when she sees Harrison enter the room. She sits up in bed.

"Hey beautiful," says Harrison as he lies across the bed.

"Is Hassa asleep?" asks Chutney.

"Yes, my dad is holding her," says Harrison.

"You guys are going to spoil her," says Chutney with a smile.

"Yes we are she is the first girl in my family other than my mom," says Harrison with a smile.

"I can see now she is gonna be a mess," says Chutney.

"Don't you worry I take care of my girls and my little man. He seems to have gotten more active since the baby," says Harrison.

"I noticed as it got closer to me having her he needed more and more attention," says Chutney.

"As long as your mom is here, believe me he is getting all the attention he needs," says Harrison.

"My mom is more partial to boys," informs Chutney.

"Baby can you please go and get Hassa I want to see her," says Chutney.

"Okay," says Harrison and he leave to go and get her.

After a few short moments Harrison walks into the room carrying her.

"Hey sweetie, they been passing you around down there like a loaf of bread," says Chutney as she reaches for Hassa.

Hassa makes cooing noises.

"Isn't she the most beautiful thing you have ever seen?" asks Harrison.

"She sure is," says Chutney as she kisses Hassa on the forehead.

Harrison lies on the bed next to Chutney. He puts his phone down on the bed and admires his wife admiring their newborn.

"Baby I am tired," says Harrison as he yawns.

"Take a nap," says Chutney as she cuddles the baby.

She slides down in the bed and lays Hassa between the two of them.

"Thanks baby," says Harrison.

"For what?" asks Chutney.

"For being beautiful and giving me beautiful kids," says Harrison then he passionately kisses her.

The three of them take a nap together before dinner.

Daniela comes into the bedroom unaware that they are taking a nap together and is happy for what she sees.

Daniela wanted to give her kids a father and a happy home, but things did not work out that way. She is happy to see that her daughter has the happily ever after. She stares at them for awhile then she quietly closes the bedroom door behind her.

Chapter Thirty Two

(Fast forward 5 years)

Harrison Jr., is now six years old and loves to play soccer and basketball while Hassa, is a bubbly five year old whom is active in ballet, soccer and dance.

Marcel, the nanny of five years is at ballet classes with Hassa then they are on their way to the soccer field to watch Harrison Jr. play. Grandma and Grandpa Devereaux are visiting along with Harrison's parents.

The restaurant continues to thrive and Chutney has made sure that revenue has almost doubled in the past five years. Chutney has more than proven herself and she knows every aspect of the business she has come a long way from the days of just being a struggling model, helping Katina with Harrison House and hostess.

Chutney expects nothing, but the best from her staff and they know it. She had to let go of Cyndi because she was coming in late all the time and a few others but they were quickly replaced.

Chutney's has become quite a success story on the West Coast. Restaurant businesses are hard to maintain, most go out of business in a year or two and sometimes less.

Harrison is very proud of Chutney and they are both happy with the work that Marcel does for them they treat her like family and the children love her.

Harrison got his way, Marcel is from Tobago and came with very high recommendations from families she had worked for in the past. She never married nor had kids of her own, therefore her schedule is flexible and she can work extra if they need her.

When ballet class is over Marcel rushes Hassa to the van that Harrison purchased for her to drive the kids to school, practices, parties and anywhere else they need to go.

When they get to the park the game has just begun.

Marcel sets up her video equipment then she and Hassa take their seats in the bleachers next to the rest of the family.

Harrison never sits in the stands he always stands at the gate and yells out instructions for Harrison Jr.

Chutney is so busy with the restaurant and rarely comes to either of the kids recitals and games, but she explains to the both of them that she has to work. Marcel videos every recital and game so that she and Harrison may review it at their leisure.

Just before the game is over Chutney arrives at the park.

"Mommy," says Hassa as she walks over to her mother with her arms stretched out.

"Hey baby, is your brother winning?" asks Chutney.

"Hi everyone," says Chutney as she walks over to Harrison and gives him a kiss.

"I am glad you were able to make it," says Harrison.

"Mommy I want a sno cone," says Hassa.

"Marcel can you take her to get a sno cone please," says Chutney.

"Sure Mrs. Allen," says Marcel.

Marcel gets up from her seat and grabs Hassa's hand to go to the refreshment stand.

Chutney takes a seat in the bleachers next to everyone else.

Harrison Jr. sees his mother take a seat in the bleachers and he has a smile on his face.

Chutney's phone rings and she excuses herself to take the call.

When the game is over Chutney is still on the phone, but she is about to get off when Harrison Jr. runs over to his father then to Marcel whom congratulates him for the win. He is looking for his mother, but he does not see her.

"Tonight I am going to make your favorite," says Grandma Gwenn to Harrison Jr.

"I want a lot of plantains," says Harrison Jr.

Marcel kisses Harrison Jr. on the cheek and he hugs her around the waist.

"Son, you did great, you are turning into an awesome soccer player," says Harrison as he kisses the top of his son's head.

"Great win Baby," says Chutney as she walks over to where everyone else is.

"You play just like your father," says Katina.

"Thanks Nana," says Harrison Jr.

"Daddy can we go and get pizza with the rest of the team?" asks Harrison Jr.

"Sure we will all go," says Harrison.

"Honey I can't I have to get back to the restaurant," says Chutney as she finishes sending a text message.

"Babe the boy just won his game and I am sure he wants his mother there," says Harrison.

"It's okay she always has to work," says Harrison Jr.

"Thank you for understanding Baby, give mommy a kiss," says Chutney.

Harrison Jr. goes to his mother and gives her a kiss.

"I'll see you guys later," says Chutney as she wave goodbye.

"I need to talk to you," says Harrison as he follows Chutney.

"About what?" asks Chutney as she walks back to her car.

"I want you to be more hands on with the kids, I know we have a nanny, but you are their mother," says Harrison in a hushed tone so that the children cannot hear him.

"Are you saying that I am not a good mother?" asks Chutney.

"I never said that Chutney, you are at the restaurant all the time and that was not the plan," says Harrison.

"I work my ass off," says Chutney as she lowers her voice when she sees people passing them.

"Harrison Jr. played a good game," says one of the parents as they pass them walking to their vehicle.

"Thanks all the kids played well today," says Harrison as he smiles at them.

"Chutney I appreciate everything you do at the restaurant, but I wanted you to be home with the kids more than you are at the restaurant," says Harrison.

"Well I can't do both and besides I love to work and I do spend time with my kids. You wouldn't know you are gone all the time," says Chutney.

"And that is why I want you home most of the time. I want you home by nine o'clock tonight. I am not coming to the restaurant and I want to finish this conversation," says Harrison.

"The restaurant doesn't close until twelve," says Chutney.

"It will be okay without you for one night," says Harrison.

"It will," says Chutney in an angry condescending tone.

Chutney says nothing she gets into her E-class sedan Mercedes and drives off.

(Later that night)

The house is quiet when Chutney walks in and she goes straight to the children's bedrooms.

She pulls the cover over Harrison Jr., smoothes his curly hair back, kisses him on the forehead and places a few of his toys back into his toy box.

She walks through the restroom and into Hassa's room and picks up some of her dolls she steps on that were left lying on the floor. She notices that Harrison is asleep in bed with Hassa, Chutney cannot see her face because her long silky dark hair is all over her face. Chutney kisses her and wakes Harrison and they both go into the master suite and close the door.

"You just getting home?" asks Harrison as he wipes the sleep from his eyes.

"Yes," says Chutney as she sits on the side of the bed and takes her Vince Camuto stilettos off.

"Baby I want you to be home with the kids, this is why I work hard so that you do not have to," says Harrison.

"Honey we have a nanny I don't see what the problem is," says Chutney.

"The problem is I had both my parents and my mother stayed at home with me as most of my friend's mothers did," says Harrison.

"Harrison you were spoiled my mother worked and hardly ever came to the school for anything for any of us and I turned out fine," says Chutney.

"I'm not saying it can't be done I am just saying that I want the mother of my kids at home. Let's make a deal you are at the restaurant five days a week, can we agree to two days a week," says Harrison.

"No, that's not enough I will be willing to cut back one day," says Chutney.

"Chutney did you notice your children go to Marcel for everything. You can be sitting right there and they will walk right past you to get to her," says Harrison.

"Well that is what they are supposed to do that is why we pay her, right?" says Chutney.

"No. We pay her to take up the slack and that is why I gave her the rest of the week off because my mom and my grandmother are here and you are going to cut back on your hours at the restaurant," says Harrison.

"You are not going to ask me, you are going to demand I cut my hours," says Chutney.

"Do you know how many women would love to be home with their kids I have some teammates with children that don't have a nanny in the home unless they have to go somewhere or when they have their charity obligations," says Harrison.

"Well I ain't them. You took modeling away from me so that I can have your children," says Chutney.

"I took it away you weren't even working. You were waitressing more than modeling," says Harrison.

"Yeah, but you knew that is what I wanted to do," says Chutney.

"You never said that I was happy with the way our life was then you got pregnant and don't get me wrong I love and adore my children, but don't act like you had a thriving career and it was cut short because you got pregnant," says Harrison.

"I can't believe you are talking to me like this," says Chutney.

"You brought it up. And another thing I found out from Marcel is that you only go to the children's events when I am home other than that you don't come. Is that true?" asks Harrison.

"So what are you doing checking up on me," says Chutney.

"I just ask her a question. I want to know what is going on when I am not here and I found out a lot," says Harrison.

"Really," says Chutney.

"Really, I want you home," says Harrison in a loud tone.

"Don't yell at me," says Chutney.

Harrison does a woosah and tries to calm himself.

"Look, I love you and I don't want this to get outta hand and besides there is something I have been wanting to talk to you about," says Harrison in a calm voice.

"What is it?" says Chutney as she finishes getting undressed.

"I want to retire I have been thinking about it and after today I know I have to, the game is not fun to me anymore. I want to be home with my family. We will be fine financially because I have seen to that," says Harrison in a sincere tone.

"Are you crazy you still have a few more years in the game," says Chutney.

"I know, but I don't want to leave the game all battered and abused. I want to come out on top of my game just like Jordan did," says Harrison.

"So what are you going to be doing commentating, coaching, motivational speaking what?" asks Chutney.

"I want to take a year or two off and take my kids to school, go on field trips with them, go to recitals and games and tuck them in bed every night," says Harrison.

"Will you be able to do that Harrison, that is a long time to be out of work," says Chutney.

"Yes. With all my investments in real estate and the restaurant, we will be fine," says Harrison as he sits down beside her to reassure her.

"I want you to continue to play," says Chutney.

"You had to know that one day my career was going to come to an end," says Harrison.

"Yes I did, but not because you want to end it," says Chutney.

"So you are saying you thought it would end by an injury," says Harrison as he moves over a little on the bed and looks at her puzzled.

"Well isn't that why most athletes get out of the game," says Chutney.

"No, Jordan left to be a business man and so has many others. You would rather I was hurt?" asks Harrison.

Chutney says nothing as she gets up to go to the restroom to take the makeup off her face.

"Answer me," says Harrison as he follows her into the restroom.

"No that's not what I am saying," says Chutney as she looks into the mirror to remove her makeup.

"Chutney I love you," says Chutney.

"I know," says Chutney.

"I want to be home with you and the kids they are growing up so fast and I want to be there. I play basketball, but basketball is not who I am Chutney," says Harrison.

"Whatever Harrison," says Chutney in a sarcastic tone. She throws away the cloth she was using to remove her makeup and walks out of the bathroom, leaving Harrison in there alone.

Chutney walks over to the bed and gets in.

Harrison turns the light off in the restroom and climbs into bed next to her.

"Look I don't want to argue," says Harrison.

"Me either," says Chutney and she turns away from Harrison on her side.

Harrison moves her curly tendrils and is kissing her on the neck.

"Harrison stop I am tired and I have a headache," says Chutney.

"Okay," says Harrison and he gets on his side of the bed and turns the lights out in the room.

The argument did not get solved and Harrison hates when they argue but he wants his kids to have the life he had. Chutney feels she was raised by a single mother and she turned out just fine, then she remembered her sister is on crack and wondered if her mother not being there for them, had anything to do with the choices her sister made in her life.

They both fall asleep, but it is a restless one.

Chapter Thirty Three

(skip ahead 2 weeks)

Chutney and Harrison are still not getting along Harrison asked that she be at the restaurant two days a week and she only cut a day, therefore she is there four days a week.

He is not happy about it, but he does not want to argue with her he actually has a surprise for tonight for them to try and rekindle their relationship. It has been a little shaky lately and he hasn't been getting any.

"Baby tonight I want to take you out , you know like a date night," says Harrison.

"I have to work," says Chutney.

"I called the restaurant and told them you won't be in tonight," says Harrison.

Chutney cuts her eyes at him.

"What are we doing, Harrison?" asks Chutney.

"I thought we could have dinner at that restaurant we went to on our first date and maybe play some games and hey maybe even catch a comedy show. I hear Mike Epps is supposed to be there tonight," says Harrison.

"I don't feel like going anywhere," says Chutney.

"Awe come on baby I am trying to make this right between us, we can't go on like this we are barely speaking to each other. You get in the bed and turn your back to me," says Harrison.

"I am just tired of you trying to control everything I do," says Chutney.

"That is not what I am trying to do I want my kids to be well rounded and I want them to be raised in a loving household," says Harrison.

Hassa walks into the den carrying her doll.

"Daddy will you have tea with me and Maggie today?" asks Hassa in a sweet tone of voice.

"Sure honey, but not for long and Mommy and I are going out, right baby," says Harrison.

"Yes. Daddy and I are going to dinner," says Chutney with a pasted on smile.

"Are me and Harrison Jr. going?" asks Hassa as she sits on her daddy's lap.

"No, not this time just me and mommy, you will be here having fun with Marcel. Maybe she can take you guys to a movie or something," says Harrison.

349

"Okay, but I want to play tea time with my dolls," says Harrison.

Harrison stands up and carries Hassa into her room for tea time.

Chutney goes to the master suite and grabs her car keys and leaves the house.

She wants to go and get a facial, mani-pedi, her hair done and makeup from the mall.

When she arrives at the mall she signs in and waits to be seen by her favorite manicurist Elsa.

"You did not make an appointment with me, how have you been," asks Elsa as she starts the water on the pedicure chair.

"I have been fine the hubby and I are going to dinner tonight and I want to look fabulous," says Chutney.

"You will you always do," says Elsa.

"How is that man of yours and the babies, why didn't you bring them I would have loved to see Ms. Hassa," says Elsa with a smile.

"Well Ms. Hassa is having tea time with her father I had to sneak out," says Chutney.

"Awe that is so sweet," says Elsa.

"No, it's funny when you see him with those long legs sitting at the little table and she puts her feathery shawls on him and he has to sip fake tea from those mini tea cups, now that's funny," says Chutney.

They both burst into laughter.

"Where is Harrison Jr.?" asks Elsa.

"He was out in the backyard playing with our nanny, Marcel," says Chutney.

"Well when you get home tell the family I said hello. Has Mrs. Katina been in town lately?" asks Elsa.

"No, I like her, but I am glad none of them has been here for at least two weeks every little thing that goes on they feel the need to fly in," says Chutney.

"You shouldn't be like that. I like having a tight knit family. Being from the Philippines we are close knit too, everybody is in everybody's business," says Elsa.

"I did not grow up like that they get on my nerves at times," says Chutney.

"All the more reason to be open to your husband's family," says Elsa as she starts to work on Chutneys feet.

"I just feel they look down on me, his grandmother hates me and his parents tolerate me," says Chutney.

"Why do you say that? I didn't see that the times when I have been around them I thought they liked you," says Elsa.

"Harrison had a little girlfriend that was the family favorite and they have never given me a chance, but I don't care anymore," says Chutney.

After getting her nails and feet done she moves into the facial room then the stylist chair to have her hair shampooed and flat ironed, then home to get ready for her night out on the town.

When Chutney arrives home, Harrison is a little upset because she did not tell him she was going out.

"Where were you?" asks Harrison in an angry tone.

"I went to get dolled up for tonight you can't tell I got my hair, nails and a facial done," says Chutney as she takes a twirl so that Harrison can look at her.

"Why didn't you tell me or bother to answer your phone?" asks Harrison.

"Because you were too busy having tea," says Chutney as she goes upstairs to shower and change.

"Harrison Jr. fell and hit his head he has a little scrape on it, can you check on him before you get dressed," says Harrison.

"Didn't you see about it? You said it was just a little scrape," says Chutney.

"Yes, Marcel put a band-aid on it because Harrison Jr. suggested it repeatedly," says Harrison.

"Okay," says Chutney.

When she gets to Harrison Jr.'s room he is on the floor playing with his toys.

"Hey I heard you had a little boo-boo today," says Chutney as she gets on the floor next to her son.

"Mommy I did not cry," says Harrison Jr.

"You didn't, you are such a big boy," says Chutney and she kisses him on the band-aid.

Harrison Jr. smiles at his mother while pushing his truck on the floor.

"I have to go and get ready I will try to be back before you go to bed," says Chutney.

"Are going to the restaurant?" asks Harrison Jr.

"No. I am going on a date with daddy tonight," says Chutney.

"Oh, is Hassa and I going?" asks Harrison Jr.

"No, just Daddy and I," says Chutney as she gets off the floor and grabs her Louis Vuitton purse.

"Gimme a kiss," says Chutney.

Harrison stands and gives his mommy a kiss. Chutney exits the room.

Soon as Chutney gets to the master suite and starts her shower Hassa comes into the room.

"Mommy I want to go," says Hassa.

Harrison enters the room.

"Daddy I want to go," says Hassa as she looks at her daddy with those beautiful brown eyes.

"Baby maybe we can," says Harrison as he was interrupted by Chutney.

"No. Hassa you know how when you play tea time with Daddy and you don't want me or Harrison Jr. to invade on your time with daddy. Well that is how I feel, I want some time with daddy by myself," says Chutney as she gets eye level with Hassa.

Chutney walks over and hits the intercom to get Marcel.

"Yes," says Marcel.

"Can you come to my room please," says Chutney.

Moments later Marcel is standing in the entrance of the master bedroom.

"Can you take Hassa to the kitchen and the two of you can bake some cookies please," says Chutney.

"Sure Mrs. Allen," says Marcel.

"Come on, Ms. Hassa let's make some chocolate chip cookies," says Marcel.

"Okay, can we put some m&m in them too?" asks Hassa.

"Yes ma'am," says Marcel.

The two of them leave the room hand in hand.

Chutney goes into the bathroom to get into the shower.

Shortly afterwards Harrison joins her.

"I want tonight to be special," says Harrison.

"I am looking forward to it," says Chutney.

Harrison kisses Chutney and this time she kisses him back, he feels the night is off to a good start.

They make love and Harrison feels the night is getting even better.

Dinner goes off without any problems and they both laughed and enjoyed each other's company, but when Harrison wants to go to another spot, Chutney reminds him that it is getting late and she has to work tomorrow and an argument ensues. Harrison reminds her that he will be retiring "Like it or not." They are right back where they started from.

Chapter Thirty Four

(a month passes)

Chutney is at the restaurant sitting at the bar taking a break when she hears her husband's voice on the television. She turns and tells the bartender to turn it up a little bit.

Harrison is sitting at a table holding a press conference.

"I am announcing today after a long and hard talk with myself, family, friends and coaches I have decided that I will be retiring after the season is over. Basketball has been good to me and my family, but I feel it is time to move on," says Harrison.

The media is going wild and the cameras are clicking fiercely as the sports announcers have their mics jammed in his face to be the first to ask him questions.

"Mrs. Allen I did not know he was thinking of retirement," says Thad the bartender.

"Uh, yeah he has mentioned it a few times. Thad tell the staff I am leaving and I'll be back tomorrow I need to take care of something," says Chutney.

"Yes ma'am, are you okay?" asks Thad.

"Yes, just do as you are told," says Chutney as she walks around the bar to get her purse and she quickly leaves the restaurant.

Chutney drives home fuming. She tries to call Harrison, but he does not answer.

"Who does he think he is, how does he make a decision like this and does not tell me," says Chutney aloud to herself. She is driving like a crazy person to get home as fast as she can.

When she arrives home she notices the van and Harrison's 600 series Benz is not in the garage.

She tries calling Harrison again, but this time she can tell he sends the call to his voice mail.

She tries Marcel's phone and she answers.

"Where the hell are you?" asks Chutney.

"Uh, at the press conference for Mr. Allen with the kids," says Marcel.

"Where at?" asks Chutney.

"At the news station, WEEZ," states Chutney.

"Where is my husband?" asks Chutney in an annoyed voice.

"He is talking to the media," says Marcel.

"Is he still on the air?" asks Chutney.

"No ma'am we will be leaving soon," says Marcel.

"Put his behind on the phone," yells Chutney.

Marcel gets Harrison's attention he walks over and hands Hassa to her.

"Who is it?" asks Harrison.

"It's your wife," says Marcel with a funny look on her face.

"Can you take the kids to the car I will meet you guys at home," says Harrison. He gives the kids a kiss and says goodbye.

"Yes," says Harrison into the phone.

"What the hell is going on?" asks Chutney.

"What do you mean?" asks Harrison.

"You had a press conference to announce your retirement and your wife was not there," says Chutney in a loud tone.

"I have been trying to tell you and you haven't been talking to me so what was I supposed to do. I have an obligation to my team," says Harrison.

"You have an obligation to your wife," says Chutney.

"I thought so too, but my wife is not talking to me and whenever I bring up my retirement she doesn't want to talk about it," says Harrison.

"I didn't want you to do it," says Chutney.

"Look I will be home soon, I am not about to get into this with you. See you soon," says Harrison as he pushes the end button on Marcel's cellular phone.

Chutney looks at her cell phone in total astonishment.

"I cannot wait until he gets home," says Chutney to herself.

Chutney goes upstairs, puts on a pair of sweat pants and a T-shirt and patiently waits on him and the kids to get home.

Chutney hears the garage door open up she goes to the door and it is Marcel with the kids.

"Mommy did you see daddy on television today?" asks Harrison Jr.

"Yes I did," says Chutney.

"We went to the television station," states Hassa.

"I know and you look so pretty," says Chutney as she kisses Hassa on the forehead.

"Where is Harrison?" asks Chutney.

"He is coming," says Marcel.

"Can you take the kids upstairs and change their clothes please?" asks Chutney.

"Yes ma'am," says Marcel.

A few moments later Chutney hears a car pull into the garage.

Harrison comes into the house. "Hey," says Harrison.

"So what are you going to do now?"

"I am going to finish out the season,"

"Then what?"

"I don't know I will have a year or two to think about it, but I know I am going to finish my master's in business and I don't know what else Chutney."

"You should have told me Harrison you had me looking like a fool."

"No, I didn't. I tried to talk to you, but you don't listen. I remember when we first got together we would have long talks about our future and now everything is about you."

"I want to have a life separate from just being your wife."

"What are you saying? You don't want to be my wife?"

"I never said that. What I said was I am trying to be Chutney, not just Harrison of the L.A. Clipper's wife."

"What is wrong with that, many women out there would love that title."

"I am trying to make something of myself Harrison, nothing in life is guaranteed."

"I have taken care of you and given you everything a woman could want. I don't know what else would make you happy?"

"I just didn't plan for things to turn out this way."

"What do you mean?"

"I feel trapped."

"By what? Who?"

"By this life. I am so tired of people being nice to me because I am your wife. I see how your friends and family look at me because I am uneducated. I heard your grandmother say when she thought I wasn't listening; the only thing I bring to the table is some beautiful kids."

"Chutney if you want to go back to school, go I am all for that, we can even go together."

"I hated school, I don't want to go back."

"Well don't blame anyone else because you don't have a college degree."

Chutney just drops her head.

"I did not grow up with money like you, I married into it. Harrison I don't ever want to be poor again. I don't want to wear someone else's clothes and shoes, because I didn't have anything nice to wear of my own."

"Chutney you won't."

"You're right, I won't."

"You will have to trust me on that."

"I don't trust NO man. People divorce all the time I am not like you. I am glad my children will always have and never have to worry about money."

"I didn't know you didn't trust me, I thought we were a team. Chutney, it really hurts me that you feel that way. I have taken care of you all these years and I have never let you down and now you tell me you don't trust me."

"I just mean I have always had to rely on myself."

Harrison looks at her as if he can see inside her.

"You are so self-centered and selfish. This is how you talk to me, after I have put you and the kids first in my life for the past few years."

Harrison leaves the living room and goes upstairs.

Dinner was quiet. Harrison fell asleep before Chutney came to bed. She read the kids a book and put them down by herself without the help of Marcel, she was given the night off.

When Chutney got into bed that night she crawled in naked, woke Harrison and made mad passionate love to him without a word spoken between them. The both of them want to put an end to their differences.

Chapter Thirty Five

(3 months later)

Harrison left yesterday for his last game of the season as an L.A. Clipper and Chutney and the kids are expected to arrive today for the game and the retirement ceremony.

Chutney has been packing and she has given Marcel a week off, she bought a ticket for her to go back to Tobago to visit her family for awhile.

Everything is almost packed when she goes into her room and sees the shoebox from when she first met Harrison and he bought her a pair of Louis Vuitton patent leather pumps. She looks in the box and slides them on her feet and remembers that day she was so happy to have them.

She has several pairs of them as well as other brand name shoes and clothes to last her a lifetime. She takes the Louis Vuittons she got on her first date with Harrison downstairs.

Chutney and the kids leave the house and lock the door behind them. When Chutney gets into the limousine she has a smile on her face and tells the kids how much she loves them and they drive off.

(The next afternoon)

Harrison pulls up to his home and he gets an eerie feeling, he runs into the house.

When he opens the door he hears an echo because all of his furniture is gone and so is his family.

"Hassa, Chutney, Harrison Jr."

No one answers he has been trying to get Chutney on the phone since last night but to no avail.

His mom and dad wanted to come to the house with him, but he told them to go home and now he wishes he had told them to come because he feels so alone.

He calls Chutney's phone again.

"Hello, what do you want?"

"What do you mean what do I want, where are you and where are my kids?"

They are fine we are at the Four Seasons if you want to speak to me talk to my lawyer, Mr. Kendall. Go into the kitchen there is something on the island for you."

Chutney hangs up the phone.

Harrison runs into the kitchen where he sees the shoes he bought Chutney on their first date sitting atop a manila envelope.

When he opens the envelope he sees divorce papers and the business card to an attorney, Mr. Kendall a divorce attorney that is representing Chutney.

Harrison is filled with rage, anger, sadness and loneliness.

He goes to the Four Seasons hotel and tries to get her room number, but the staff has been put on alert to not let him up. He did not create a scene, but he was demanding that she come downstairs and talk to him, therefore security and the police were called and he was escorted off the property without incident.

On the news the next day they reported he was being irate, security had to calm him down and he did thousands of dollars in damage to the lobby area.

He tries several more times to call Chutney and she does not answer, Harrison spends the rest of the night wondering what is going on and what can he do to fix it.

(2 weeks later)

Harrison has retained an attorney and they are in mediation. When he sees Chutney walk in with her attorney he stands.

"Chutney what is wrong? Whatever it is I can fix it," says Harrison with tears in his eyes. He has not spoken to Chutney since this drama began because she won't talk his calls nor has he seen his kids.

"You are what is wrong did you really think I could be with you look at me and look at you. Did you really think I could be with you? You scare me sometimes because of how ugly you are," says Chutney.

Her attorney taps her on the shoulder to try to tell her to be quiet.

"What are you saying?" asks Harrison.

"I just wanted your money. I never loved you, but I tried," says Chutney.

Harrison looks at her in disbelief.

"You cannot tell me you never loved me that you were just faking it," says Harrison.

"Yes, I was until I couldn't do it anymore," says Chutney.

"I was a good husband to you I gave you a good life you ungrateful women," says Harrison.

"I may be ungrateful, but you are still ugly and next time stay in your lane. Marry a woman that is a two, because without money you would have never been able to bag this," says Chutney in a nasty tone.

"Mrs. Allen we are not kids here let's not name call," says Harrison's attorney, Mrs. Lumpkin.

"I will call him whatever I want," says Chutney.

"We are here to get a clear understanding of what the marital assets are and find out what does each party want to take from the marriage once it is dissolved," says Mr. Kendall, Chutney's attorney.

"I want everything and make sure to note that there is no pre-nup in place," says Chutney as she sits back in her white leather chair.

Harrison looks at his attorney.

"Don't' worry about that we can contest it," whispers Mrs. Lumpkin.

"Chutney we can work through this, we need to talk," says Harrison as he licks his dry pink peeling lips. Then he pulls a piece of skin off of them.

"See that is what I am talking about, did you see what he just did. He repulses me," says Chutney.

"I don't think that is a good idea," warns Mr. Kendall.

"I ain't giving her nothing, I will take care of my kids, which I want custody of because as you all can see she only cares about herself," says Harrison.

"Where are my kids?" asks Harrison.

"They are with Marcel at the hotel," says Chutney with a grin.

"My client has the right to see his children he has not seen them in two weeks," informs Mrs. Lumpkin.

"He can see them today as long as he is calm and keeps the kids out of this mess," says Chutney.

"What time do they get out of school?" asks Mrs. Lumpkin.

"At three," says Chutney as she crosses her legs.

"I want to pick them up from school," offers Harrison.

"Mr. Allen will pick the kids up today from school and he will return them to their mother bv six o'clock p.m. today," says Mrs. Lumpkin.

"Do you agree to that Mrs. Allen?" asks Mr. Kendall.

Chutney nods her head.

"She has taken all the furniture and art from the walls," adds Harrison.

"I want the boat, the restaurant and I want the money to buy myself a home like the one we shared as husband and wife," says Chutney with a smug look on her face.

"She did not buy any of that stuff and when I met her she was sleeping in her friend's loft. She didn't even have a car," informs Harrison as he looks around the room.

"That may be true Mr. Allen, but have you heard of when you bring someone especially a spouse into a certain lifestyle you have to keep them in that lifestyle," states Mr. Kendall

"This is not fair I feel as if I am inside of a nightmare," states Harrison.

"We are willing to give Mr. Allen every other week visitation until the marriage is dissolved or the judge states otherwise," states Mr. Kendall.

"Do you agree with that Mr. Allen?" asks Mrs. Lumpkin.

"I want to see my kids every day. I spent more time with the kids than she did, she was always working. She only wants them to get more money out of me," says Harrison in an angry tone.

"Let's not talk about how much you were gone. I ran the house, the restaurant and Harrison House most of the time," says Chutney.

"We will need a statement of all Mr. Allen's investments, properties and holdings," states Mr. Kendall.

"We don't have to bring a statement from my bank because she literally cleaned that out she left me a measly thousand dollars and after looking over my financial statements for the restaurant she has been skimming money from there and ain't no telling what else she has stolen," says Harrison.

"As you know in a marriage any monies gained during the marriage belongs to the both of you and is considered community property, therefore it is her's to take," says Mr. Kendall.

"That account had approximately forty thousand in it and she left me one thousand dollars. The restaurant account had over two hundred thousand in it she left me five thousand dollars. The account we used for unexpected expenses had over six hundred thousand in it and she took it all, but a thousand dollars," informed Harrison.

"We have that paperwork for you as well," says Mrs. Lumpkin.

"I have got to get outta here I feel like I can't breathe," says Harrison as he loosens his tie.

Harrison gets up to walk out and all of a sudden he lunges at Chutney and she moves just in time and he misses her. He knocks over a table and leaves the room.

Chutney is yelling for someone to call the police she wants to file assault charges against Harrison.

Her attorney, Mr. Kendall is trying to calm her down. Mrs. Lumpkin goes after her client.

(one week later)

Harrison flies home to Chicago to be with his family, during this terrible time in his life.

Grandma Gwenn is there cooking all his favorite foods, though he has no appetite.

"I told you that girl was no good for you Harrison, you could just tell. I never trusted her," says Grandma Gwenn as she fixes him some soup.

"Grandma I really thought she loved me," says Harrison.

"I know. She had your mom and dad fooled too," says Grandma Gwenn.

Katina walks into the kitchen and gives Harrison a hug.

"How are you feeling today baby?" asks Katina.

"A little better, I actually woke up hungry," says Harrison.

"Well that is always a good sign," says Katina as she gives him a smile.

"Good morning Momma," says Katina.

"I need to go to the store later Katina," says Gwenn.

"Okay after we eat we can go then," says Katina.

"I am going to go for a run," says Harrison as he excuses himself from the table.

"Is there anything particular you want for dinner?" asks Grandma Gwenn.

"Stewed Chicken with peas, rice and plantains," says Harrison.

Harrison gives his Grandma and mother a kiss, a hug and left to go for a jog..

The air is crisp and Harrison is enjoying being at home, it reminds him of life before his nightmare began.

As he is jogging a car passes him, but then it stops and the windows come down.

It is Bahari.

"Hey, I didn't know you were home," says Bahari.

"Yeah, I got home day before yesterday, you know things were getting crazy," says Harrison as he looks down at his gloves.

"Yeah I know, I have been watching the T.V.," says Bahari.

"You back at home now?" asks Harrison.

"Yes, I've been back for awhile now. I am doing my residency here. Hey you want to jump in and we can go to my house and talk," says Bahari.

Harrison agrees and opens the door to her black Cadillac CTS Sedan.

When they arrive at her parent's house they are home alone.

Bahari offers him something to drink, but Harrison declines.

They sit on the sofa in the den.

"Is this new furniture?" asks Harrison.

"As a matter of fact it is," says Bahari.

"I am really sorry that you are going through all this craziness. How are you?" asks Bahari as she takes a sip of her coffee.

"I am just taking it one day at a time."

"How are your kids? What are their names again I have seen pictures and they are so adorable."

"Harrison Jr. is seven and Hassa, my little princess is five."

"Wow, how time flies."

"I just cannot make sense of this whole mess. I just want my kids and hopefully I will get them in the divorce. I want full custody."

"Good luck."

"Bahari you know I never meant to hurt you right? Can you believe the stuff she is saying about me. She acts as if I meant nothing to her."

"For her to go on television and say the things she is saying she never did. I knew you were not going to be married to her forever. I heard how she was disrespectful to your grandmother."

"They never got along, but I tried."

"You know we don't play that in our culture, we respect our elders."

"I know, but she is not from our culture."

"What are you going to do know?"

"I am probably going to move back to Chicago soon. I want when the kids come to visit that they are around my parents and grandparents."

"That's good, maybe I will get to meet them one day."

"For sure, I would like that."

"When you came to my wedding I had a feeling then that I may be making a mistake, but I loved her."

"You cheated on me and that hurt for a long time. It was hard to see you with someone else."

"We can try and rekindle our friendship and maybe go on a few dates see what happens."

"Harrison let me say something to you. When we were in middle school I was teased about the way you look, but that did not bother me. When we went to high school the teasing got worse and I still didn't care because I loved you. Behind your back they called you the tall version of Flava Flav."

"You never told me that, why?"

"Because Harrison when you love someone it is not about what they look like, it's about how you feel about them. You made a mistake and married the wrong woman, I had your back no matter what and I would have had your ugly babies and I mean that in a joking way."

"I am sorry."

"You went after the typical light-skinned model type with the long pretty hair and I mean that lightly because all textures of hair are beautiful, but I was not light enough for you. Did you think for a moment that if you were broke she would have given you the time of day?"

"I never really thought about it."

"Really Harrison, you are the only one that did not see it. It was clear for anyone that saw you guys together she was in it for the money."

"She really played me, but if she thinks she is going to get all my money and my kids, she is crazy."

"So you are still delusional. Is it true that you married her without a pre-nup?"

Harrison is quiet then he looks up at her and responds.

"Yes, but I didn't know she was a gold digger."

"Harrison that is not fair, a lot of athletes say that, but come on, you got what you paid for."

Harrison is quiet because he knows Bahari is telling him the truth and only Bahari would talk to him in such a raw and uncut way.

"You really loved her, didn't you?"

"I did, but can we be friends?"

"Yes, always."

"Can I have a hug?"

The two embrace and when Harrison releases her he grabs both her hands and is about to kiss them when he sees a ring on her ring finger.

"What is this?"

"It's my engagement ring."

"When did this happen?"

"Last weekend."

"To who?"

"Pierre."

"Do I know him? Why does that name sound familiar to me?"

"Yes you do. Remember him from Duke University."

"Oh yeah, are you about to marry that guy?"

"Yes, I am. I love him very much and he loves me."

"He had a reputation of being a womanizer in college. All the ladies liked him, probably because he had those hazel eyes."

"He still does."

"Have   you   set   a   date   yet?"
"No."

"Were you seeing him when I went to L.A.?"

"I cannot believe you are asking me that, you cheated on me remember?"

"And I am sorry about that."

There is a knock on the door.

Bahari goes to answer it.

"Hey baby, what are you doing here?"

"I came to bring my baby those bagels you love so much from downtown."

The two kiss.

"There is someone here I want you to meet."

"Who?"

"It's Harrison, remember him."

"How can I forget."

When they walk into the den area, Harrison stands.

"Hey man, how are you doing?" says Harrison.

"I'm good. What brings you to Chicago?" asks Pierre.

"Needed to come back to my roots, you know going through a rough time right now with the divorce and everything," states Harrison.

"I heard about that, sorry to hear that," says Pierre.

"Remember I told you Harrison grew up around the corner from here," says Bahari.

"Yeah I remember. Did she tell you we are getting married?" asks Pierre.

"Yes, she did. Congratulations," says Harrison.

"I moved here to follow my baby. I am so proud of her she is almost done with her residency then we are going to get married, hopefully you will be able to attend," says Pierre.

"Where are you from?" asks Harrison.

"New York," says Pierre as he looks at Bahari and gives her a kiss.

"Hey, I am going to get outta here and finish my run," says Harrison.

"You want me to give you a ride back?" asks Bahari.

"No, I need the exercise. Congratulations again and Bahari I'll see you later," says Harrison.

"I'll walk you out," says Bahari.

When they get to the door Harrison hesitates and looks at Bahari with a smile.

"I should have known someone would sweep you off your feet, you deserve it. You know what they say: you snooze, you lose."

"True. If you ever want to talk, just call me," says Bahari.

"You are still nice to me even though I did you wrong," says Harrison.

"I am nice to my friend, not the person that broke my heart," says Bahari.

The two of them embrace. Harrison leaves and Bahari closes the door behind him. As he is running the tears start to well up in his eyes. Bahari is the woman that should have been Mrs. Allen.

Because he was captivated by Chutney's looks he was tricked, like a devil in sheep's clothing. Looking back he realizes that Chutney had a plan all along. She manipulated him with sex. Chutney had him where he couldn't think straight.

Harrison wondered if Bahari was still a virgin, but he knew he had no right to ask. Harrison stops for awhile to try to get his mind right to finish his jog, but he starts to sob uncontrollably.

Harrison's life was a mess and it was going to be a process to get things straightened out and live a quiet private life again.

(Meanwhile)

When Bahari returns to the living room Pierre was flipping channels on the television he stops when he sees Chutney on the Wendy Williams Show discussing the divorce.

Chutney is going on and on about how ugly he is, how his breath stunk and that she was going to take him for every penny he has. Chutney has been on all the talk shows that will have her, every rag magazine, Twitter, Facebook, and Instagram.

When asked by Wendy Williams did she ever love Harrison her response was, "I didn't allow myself to, I was all about the money. He got what he wanted which was a beautiful woman on his arm and I got the house, kids, cars and most of the money."

Wendy with her index finger waves for the cameras to come in closer and zoom in on her face says, "Nah, how you doing?"

The audience and Chutney burst into laughter.

Other Books by
Sa'Neal

Poppa

Goodbye Patrick

Scarlet Thread

Please visit booksbysaneal.com

CPSIA information can be obtained
at www.ICGtesting.com
Printed in the USA
FFOW04n1909150816
26753FF